KU-043-630

CAPTAIN OF THE CARYATID

Captain Septimus Macready, commander of the lighthouse tender *Caryatid,* presides over the peaceful Celtic port of Port Ardur, while for second officer Charlie Farthing, it feels as though he has found the home he's always dreamt of. James St John Stanier, newly appointed Harbour Master, is ambitious and determined to make his mark and wears his authority on his sleeve. In this unique novel of seamanship, rivalry and romance, the *Caryatid*'s course and the Harbour Master's ambitions move towards collision on the lovely island of Ynyscraven, second home to the *Caryatid*'s crew.

CAPTAIN OF THE CARYATID

CAPTAIN OF THE CARYATID

by
Richard Woodman

Magna Large Print Books
Long Preston, North Yorkshire,
England.

British Library Cataloguing in Publication Data.

Woodman, Richard
    Captain of the Caryatid.

    A catalogue record for this book is
    available from the British Library

    ISBN 0-7505-1317-9

First published in Great Britain by Severn House Publishers
Ltd., 1997

Copyright © 1997 by Richard Woodman

Cover illustration by arrangement with Severn House
Publishers Ltd.

The moral right of the author has been asserted

Published in Large Print 1998 by arrangement with Severn
House Publishers Ltd.

All rights reserved. No part of this publication may be
reproduced, stored in a retrieval system, or transmitted in any
form or by any means, electronic, mechanical, photocopying,
recording or otherwise, without the prior permission of the
Copyright owner.

Magna Large Print is an imprint of
Library Magna Books Ltd.
Printed and bound in Great Britain by
T.J. International Ltd., Cornwall, PL28 8RW.

All situations in this publication are fictitious and any resemblance to living persons is purely coincidental.

For the ship's company of the lighthouse
tender *Alert,* and the keepers of the
lighthouses at Lundy,
1967–1970

Contents

Contents

A Quiet Sunday Evening

Captain Septimus Macready dozed in front of the fire. His consciousness swam slowly from its refuge among the foggier recesses of his brain towards the warm reality of a Sunday evening. It was the incessant clicking of knitting needles that compelled him to abandon his reverie.

The knitting needles belonged to his wife. The recollection brought him back to full consciousness. He surreptitiously opened both eyes and without moving his head stared from under his brows across the hearth.

Opposite the Captain the small bird-like person of Mrs Gwendolen Macready sat with the immobility of a coiled spring. The Captain regarded his wife. Their marriage had existed for twenty-three years. For twenty-two of them, matrimony had resembled the lines of a railway track,

11

running smoothly parallel, interdependent as an entity yet independent in part.

There had been romance; a brief, intense experience that had forged a mutual link between the two, then faded, leaving them individual and only slightly, guiltily, dependent upon each other. Thus their twin lives ran abreast, the distance between them impeccably exact, an absolute constant.

The Captain's eye roved over his wife: the sensible slippers, lisle stockings and plaid skirt; the cardigan and glasses retained by a bight of cord around her neck. He watched her nimble hands click-click the needles as she knitted yet another woollen garment for the interminable children that Porth Ardur produced.

Captain Macready closed his eyes again and sighed gently. Children. Maybe that was the trouble. They had never had any children. Neither was wholly to blame yet each bore a fragment of guilt and it was an unmentioned barrier between them. The Captain wondered what it was really like to be a parent. Most of his crew were. Mrs Morgan was.

At the thought of Justine Morgan and her daughter his heart kindled. The widow was everything his wife was not. She was brassy, drank gin and laughed explosively. Where his wife's brownish hair was greying, Justine Morgan's became blacker. Her ample bosom conveyed an infinite prospect of comfort and her thick, well-formed legs carried her stockily voluptuous frame with a pride that busy Mrs Macready dismissed as vulgar self-indulgence.

Mrs Morgan was the Captain's official dancing partner. Between them they had carried off several local trophies and were hopeful of completing their repertoire by collecting the regional prize for Latin American dancing that winter.

At the thought of dancing with Mrs Morgan Captain Macready smiled slyly to himself. He had never stepped, nor ever attempted to step, beyond the strictest bounds of propriety in five years. In a way this added a piquancy to his relationship with the widow who had, whilst yielding in the most sensuous embrace of the dance, never sought to encourage the Captain's attentions extramurally. In the town Mrs Morgan was considered 'fast', a largely unjust judgement by those jealous of her way of life. In truth it was as unkind as it was incorrect for despite her apparent sociability in The Feathers, dancing was her pleasure and the adornment of her own body her especial vice.

In a curious way the Captain and Mrs Morgan were ideally suited partners. They were both short, stocky and well-formed, inclined to a middle-aged thickening, but healthily and athletically confident in their own physical power. They therefore danced well and had recently been chosen by their team-mates as Porth Ardur's leading couple.

Mrs Macready viewed her husband's dancing with cool rationality. He had, after all, a certain social position to maintain in Porth Ardur and he was a fine figure of a man, setting off a brass bound uniform or evening dress extremely well. Gwendolen Macready was a pragmatist from her plaid skirt to her avuncular attitude towards her husband's dancing, with a sense of purpose that enabled her to ignore such innuendoes that the Captain's choice of partner had fostered. Besides in five years they had died down, having nothing—beyond malicious speculation—to feed upon. Mrs Macready considered her husband deserved some pleasure and seemed content that he was, himself, contented. After all, he was a sailor and the dancing provided sufficient innocent evidence to support the romantic image his profession had acquired. Besides, it allowed her to support a slightly martyred attitude as much as it gave her freedom to preside in the town as the Captain's Lady and attend the organisations she enjoyed.

These were the Ladies' Circle, the Mothers' Union, Women's Institute, the League of Hospital Friends, etc, etc, for the list was apparently endless. None, she quietly asserted to herself, could function without her tireless energy. Gwendolen Macready was one of Porth Ardur's Principal Wives, one of those powers behind the various thrones in the little seaport's hierarchy that knew that they, and they alone, made the town function at the human level. Certainly their husbands might occupy the offices of Town Clerk, Mayor, Chief Inspector of Constabulary, Estate Agent, Rector, Collector of Customs and so forth but it was their wives who exercised influence and guided affairs into the 'proper' channels.

Within this structure Gwendolen Macready occupied a unique niche, for she was *the* Captain's wife of Porth Ardur. Oh, there were many sons of the town who earned their livings at sea, every street boasted at least one Board of Trade Certificate. Many still lived in the town, or at least their wives and families did, having married local girls with the homing instinct of the true sailor. Many too were masters of merchant ships, captains in their own right, but they were not the Captain known best in Porth Ardur.

That distinction was indisputably held by Septimus Macready, Master of the Lighthouse Tender *Caryatid* which, with all its 900 gross registered tons, dominated the tiny granite inner harbour of Porth Ardur at weekends. The *Caryatid* berthed regularly on Friday as the tide served for, as the Bosun never failed to remind the Carpenter as the steamer warped into her berth: 'There'll be dancin' tonight, Chippy!'

Bernard Foster, First Mate of the *Caryatid*, threw the last wall-eyed, one-legged teddy bear into the wooden box and thankfully slammed the lid shut. He collapsed into a chair and stoked up his pipe as the gurglings of his children, subsiding into sleep, floated down to him from upstairs.

His wife, haggard with the effort of trying to bath two robust boys, entered the room. She too slumped into a chair.

'I'll make a pot of tea,' she muttered, closing her eyes.

'Don't worry, I'll do it,' he answered. For a long while neither moved.

'Monday tomorrow,' she said at last.

'M'm.' He agreed with the obvious, knowing the implications in the trite remark. Monday meant him being away at sea until Friday. It was not long but Anthea Foster groaned mentally at the prospect: the two boys, four evenings on her own, it was enough to wilt the strongest spirit. She thought of something else.

'You'll be tired next weekend, I suppose?' She got up from her chair.

'Sorry?' He looked up at her, uncomprehending, seeing her fading good looks sadly heightened by her exhaustion.

'You'll be working extra next week with Barry gone.' Her reference to the Second Mate, who had that week decided to rush off and ship out on a tanker, brought comprehension to him.

'Oh that, sorry love, no you don't have to worry: there's a new chap coming down on the overnight train, name of Farthing, Charles Farthing ... ' He puffed his pipe. 'Going to make tea?' She nodded, brushing a wisp of hair back from her forehead. There was more than a touch of grey in it, he noted wistfully. Oh well, one could only bow to the inevitable, but it was a shame that such a beauty as Anthea should wither so soon ...

She came back into the room with a tray.

'It's an odd coincidence. I mean, Porth Ardur so rarely has any new faces that to get two in the same week is a real bonus ...' She tried to smile.

'Two?' said her husband.

'Yes, Mrs Humphries told me that the new Harbour Master was expected this Monday. She's been cleaning for old Captain Edwardes' widow; such a pity about him, he was such a gentleman ...'

'Mmmmm,' agreed her husband, emitting clouds of aromatic blue smoke.

Charles Farthing was not, as his name tended to imply, a round man. He was an extremely gaunt twenty-year-old with a penchant for cavalry twills and shapeless sweaters which gave him the appearance of an itinerant scarecrow. Some two hours after the conversation between Mr and Mrs Foster, Charlie was struggling out of a taxi in the capital's west-bound railway terminus cursing the rain. Behind his cab another drew up and from this stepped out a man little older than Charlie but in an immaculate suit. With an instinct peculiar to such persons, the porters who were dubiously approaching Charlie switched their attention to the newer arrival and, with the motivation of true snobs, unloaded the man's baggage. As the two taxis drove away Charlie was still standing in the rain cursing.

Unbeknown to the two men they were the very persons Anthea Foster had been discussing, for the immaculate gentleman was Porth Ardur's new Harbour Master. He was an ambitious fellow, one of that professional breed of mariners that go ashore early and, having the right background and the right connections, become authorities upon matters maritime, write books about the sea and ultimately become consulted for dreadful films about seafaring. They studiously insist on being called 'Captain', though frequently commanding nothing more manoeuvrable than a large mahogany desk. Such was the man destined to become Harbour Master of the little Celtic port of Porth Ardur. His name, if we ignore his self-styled title, was James St John Stanier.

While Stanier was being tenderly tucked into his extortionate first class sleeper, Charlie was struggling down the platform in search of a third class compartment empty enough for him to occupy a whole banquette in a horizontal position. When he eventually found one and had stowed his cases he was running in perspiration. He therefore decided to indulge himself in a little ritual he used to perform as a child. He strolled casually down the platform until he reached the locomotive. Then he inspected the gleaming beast, its green paint throwing back the platform lights, steam rising from the piston glands and a wisp of smoke from the funnel. He read the locomotive's number and the name in brass letters over the wheel arch: 'King Charles I'. Was that a good or a bad omen? Good for Charlie Farthing or a dismal reference to the doomed King? He turned away and stared ahead to where the lines, catching the yellow station lights, tangled in points beneath the gaudy reds and greens of the signal gantry, then straightened out into the four tracks that faded into dark distance. The magic iron road to the West. He muttered the word in the gloom, pleased with its sibilance. He had a faerie image of towering cliffs with Tintagel-like fortresses defying the Atlantic swells, of mists and maidens and wind-buffeted trees clawing for existence against the southwesterlies that scoured the rugged coast. Was it the land of dragons, of Merlin and the legendary Arthur? He chuckled inwardly at himself. Cynicism rose up in him. Why did he always dream these stupid romantic dreams? He had been at sea for eight years and still, if he was going somewhere he had not previously visited, thought that this might be the place where legend and fact mingled in a dream-like reality to which he could surrender his soul and settle.

As he walked back to his compartment he remembered that first, shattering blow to his preconceived notions. For two months he had listened to his shipmates' stories about the beauty of Japanese women. He had been sixteen, on his first voyage, receptive to every emotive chord anyone wished to pluck. He had augmented these tales with fantasies. At last the ship berthed and at last young Charlie got ashore. He swaggered into a bar in Izesaki-Cho and an almond-eyed beauty of indescribable delicacy had sat beside him. She had gazed longingly into his eyes, bathed his hands and face in hot, scented towels and brushed her sandalwood scented hair in black waves across his cheek. As she spoke Charlie fell in love and as she stroked his thigh he felt the heat of passion combine with an unbearable crescendo of longing. 'Are you cherry-boy?' she had asked. Charlie could not believe such poetic imagery existed in speech, used as he was to a terse Saxon formality. But this was the land of cherry blossom, this was the Orient, the Mystic East. He nodded, transported with happiness.

'I love you for free ...'

Charlie's breath was coming in ecstatic sobs. His cheek was being stroked, the girl's nails scratching it with the same delicacy one taps porcelain, her other had found that hitherto innocent part of him that was now betraying him shamefully. He surrendered, suddenly aware that the girl's breasts were pressing into him, perfumed orbs of the most celestial delights.

'I love you for free ... free fousand yen?'

Charlie was laughing as the train pulled out of the station. As it came clear of the great arch of the terminus he saw the sky was clearing. The rain had stopped and over the jumbled roofs of the capital rose a yellow moon. Orbs, mused Charlie. Those bloody orbs ... and he began to settle himself for the night.

Further down the train James St John Stanier also saw the moon. He leant nonchalantly out of the window, smoking a last cigar before retiring.

Spring tides, he thought, musing on the technical details of the port upon which he was determined to stamp his personality. Lunitidal intervals, maximum rise and fall, the neap range, the off-lying dangers to the port ... he turned over the technical data in his mind. Navigational aids ... he was not too sure what existed on that score ... at any rate there was bound to be some room for improvement. After all, there was that pier called on the chart 'Lighthouse Pier'. Odd that, because there was no light upon it other than the statutory two fixed reds that appeared on all such projections. He tossed the cigar into the darkness and pulled his head in. He was looking forward to tomorrow immensely. It was all such a tremendous challenge.

The same moon that rose over the capital shone down upon Porth Ardur. As the night wore on it cleared the shadow of Mynydd Uchaf from the sleeping town, bathing it in light. It woke Justine Morgan from her favourite dream and she lay a while trying to recover the lost shreds of happiness. She had been dreaming of her late husband, Brian Morgan. A pillar of a man with the vitality of a bull, eager as a lover, strong without roughness and yet with such a well of softness within him that his sudden death in a mining accident had left his devoted wife with a lasting image of immortality. It was as though the removal of the physical presence of his body had only been a metamorphosis. Brian Morgan remained eternally enshrined within the remembered gentlenesses of his person and these he had passed to his wife to cherish forever.

Justine smiled in the darkness. It was impossible to explain to others. That was why she had come here, twenty miles from her mining village, as a widow. Why she had stayed a widow, earning herself a decent and reasonable living first as the assistant and later as the successor to a lady who ran a small business selling garments to the ladies of Porth Ardur. But Justine remained in love with her husband, devoted to a memory that would not fade with age. That was why she held herself not only with the confidence of youth but with the certainty of experience. That was why she did what, in the eyes of other women in the town was reprehensible: she 'preserved herself'. But there was only a kind of radiant joy in this vice. For Justine Morgan preserved not only the voluptuousness of her own body by her onanistic ministrations, but the infinitely delightful sensuous memory of a vigorous and tender lover.

The moon poured into the bedroom and Justine Morgan rolled languorously onto her back. Her black mane was caught up in a scarlet ribbon, pale in the moonlight. Her breasts, large, still firm, spread across her rib cage under the *décolletage* of a nightdress her lady customers never saw in her window, and her hands fluttered reminiscently over a belly flat with tension.

Very slowly she moved her hands downwards and felt again the urgent insistence of Brian Morgan.

Calico Jack was aware of the moon only for its illuminant properties. The broad swathe of the Lighthouse Pier bucked in his vision, the ordered symmetry of its granite masonry impossibly distorted by the alcohol in his system. Despite the chill of the night Calico Jack wore upon his elderly, gaunt frame the full dress uniform of his trade. The white cotton peaked hat, the cotton sweatshirt and the faded blue denims of a steam ship fireman adorned his thin, sinewy body. He staggered with unerring purpose to the narrow plank that served as access to the *Caryatid*. He groped instinctively for the rope handrails and in seconds was aboard, swallowed up in the shadowed recesses of the silent ship. Below, he found the oil-lit messroom, where able seaman John Evans sat pouring a second mug of orange tea with the confidence of long practice. Evans was one of six Evanses on board but the only other John, and so was also called Jack. A keen fisherman, he was known to the ship's company as Mackerel Jack to differentiate from Calico Jack, whose unvaried clothing, always the same, always spotless, had earned him his own qualifying soubriquet.

No word was spoken by either of the men. Calico Jack sat down and drank the tea. After a little he writhed somewhat, then rose, flung himself at the ready-opened port and spewed into the night.

When he withdrew his head from the port he was paler but steadier. He wiped his mouth and, with a hand that trembled only slightly, lit the rolled cigarette that Mackerel offered him. Then he lurched out of the messroom and disappeared. Seconds later Mackerel heard the clang of the boiler room door and the rasp of a shovel as Calico Jack revived the banked fires in *Caryatid*'s Scotch boilers. When the sun came up Calico Jack was stone cold sober, the alcohol sweated out of him. A dark haze rose from the tall vertical funnel of the *Caryatid* and a white wisp of steam showed that the ship's whistle gland was still leaking. But it had done so as long as anyone could remember and now it no longer seemed important.

Matters of Routine

It was not immediately apparent to anyone in the town that that particular Monday morning was in any way significant in the history of Porth Ardur. There were individual beginnings but these, at the time, seemed not to impinge upon the ordered life of the sea-port.

The first to experience such an initiation was Charles Farthing. In a chilly dawn he had bundled out of the overnight express, stumbled across the junction platform and into the four-wheeled carriage of a branch line train. At a more leisurely pace, attended by a porter, James St John Stanier had traversed the same platform and, with evident distaste, sat himself down in what passed on the branch line for first class accommodation. It was not long before a pannier tank engine had been coupled up and at 6.55 a.m. it jerked out of the station.

The branch line route lay across the seaward ends of several well-defined valleys. The pithead wheels of mines showed up above the lines of small houses that ran parallel to the valleys as though stuck to the two hundred feet contour. It was a fresh spring morning, cold enough for the smoke from a thousand range fires to rise above every town through which the train progressed. At each station the train stopped. Newspapers and mail bags were flung out onto the platforms before the tank engine hissed, hooted and jerked its creaking rolling stock into further motion. Charlie was fascinated by the little towns, each isolated from the next by the massive spine of mountain into which, by way of smoky tunnels and high cuttings, the train plunged. What fascinated Charlie most was the strangeness of it all. It was as though he was in a foreign land, a sensation heightened by the unpronounceable names borne by the stations through which he passed.

After about an hour the train turned

in line with a valley and ran along its side. A mile or so later it again began to turn, bringing a stupendous view of blue water flecked with the white caps of breaking waves and shadowed darker patches where the sun threw the shadows of cumulus clouds.

For a quarter of an hour Charlie was captivated by the view. In the distance was the dim line of another shore and here and there islands, one of which bore the white column of a lighthouse which gleamed in the sunshine as though it had been of burnished metal. 'Delightful ... ' he breathed to himself and then remembered his thoughts of the previous night. A tiny tight knot of excitement began forming in the pit of his stomach. After all that globe trotting was he really about to discover a land of enchantment? Or merely a land of cynical disappointment? If a man was not meant to romanticise, why the devil was he equipped to do so? He ran his hand through his tousled hair and frowned, an annoyed and surprisingly fierce expression crossing his face.

He was interrupted from his reverie by a sudden gloom in the compartment. The train had plunged into a cutting. Sheer on either side granite rose, dripping with water, fissured by frost and time with tufts of thrift and the fresh curling green of ferns: hart's tongue and maidenhair. He was suddenly convinced that he might indeed be on the threshold of magic, some lost magic still left in the world, when the train pulled out of the cutting. Behind them, on a craggy eminence, the gaunt, fantastic outline of a castle was silhouetted black against the morning sky.

A few minutes later the train pulled into the station of Porth Ardur.

'Captain' Stanier descended from the train unaware of the morning's promise. His senses informed him that there was three eighths cloud cover of Fairweather Cumulus, that the wind was sou'west force four and that the wisp of cloud over the mountain behind him was orographic in nature and probably presaged rain. He took a taxi to the best hotel.

Captain Septimus Macready, dressed in full uniform, strode down the hill towards the harbour accumulating the same information as Stanier. In addition he also noted the state of the tide. When he reached the harbour he leaned over to look at the inner boat steps. The swell gently rose and fell, covering, then exposing two complete steps. Things did not look too good. He strode on to the ship, tossing good mornings to left and right of him as he passed fishermen and his own seamen, whom he had met here every successive Monday morning for the last decade.

Septimus Macready stepped aboard *Caryatid* noticing only details: the cleanliness of the decks, the hand-rope tension, the presence of a safety net under her gangway. Charles Farthing, arriving a few minutes later, saw the ship as a whole. She had a bar stem straight enough to rake aft when the ship trimmed by the stern. Her tiny high fo'c's'le flared outwards and then dropped abruptly to a low well-deck. This deck was dominated by the foremast which boasted two derricks. A smaller one forward, over a small hatch and a larger one aft, over an open deck. This latter seemed to be of some sort of wood, a massive spar about two feet in diameter, he guessed. At the end of the well-deck the bridge rose, abaft which a clutter of boats and tall, bell-mouthed ventilators were just visible. The bridge was high and of varnished teak with a large athwartships wheelhouse and small, open wings. At the forward end a small brass bell gleamed. He looked back at the fo'c's'le to where its partner, large, imposing and equally polished, bore the just legible legend 'CARYATID, 1910'. So the old lady was already twenty-five years old. He should have guessed, though, by the incredibly tall funnel that rose as vertically as the stem, a buff column emitting a dark heat haze from its top where, too, a wisp of white steam escaped from the whistle. Charlie was pleased with the look of the ship. She was certainly old but on that particular morning she was whimsical enough to suit his mood. He gathered up his bags for the twentieth time since leaving the station and went on board.

Stanier reached the harbour two hours later. Being a man of importance he had checked in at his hotel, changed and, having had a decent breakfast, made his way to the harbour office. It was a good time for the new Harbour Master to arrive, he reflected, as it was just coming up to high water. He patted the Admiralty tide tables a little guiltily, slightly ashamed that he needed to consult them at all. Oh, well, in a day or two it would not be necessary.

The first blow to his self-esteem came when he viewed the Harbour Office. The beautifully chiselled granite that formed Porth Ardur's sea wall and inner harbour swept seawards in two embracing arms. The outer one extended a little further in a mole to break the effects of a swell from the bay beyond. Where the two arms met, the caissons that formed the tidal gates were situated. Next to this, under the shelter of the adjacent sea wall, was an ugly, squat brick building. So eager was the new Harbour Master to sight his eyrie that he barely noticed the two coasters, half dozen fishing boats and the *Caryatid* as his taxi took him along the pier.

He was met by Thomas Jones, who was technically the Harbour Master's Coxswain but who in fact filled the offices of Dock Master, rope man and fresh water agent to ships using the port. Stanier noticed the peeling sign over the badly pointed brick work, which bore the legend 'HARBOUR MASTER, CAPT T EDWARDES, TEL: 29'.

''Aven't painted it pendin' your arrival, Cap'n,' Jones explained. Stanier was soothed by the unsolicited use of his title. He nodded curtly and went inside.

Here Jones explained that the building had been erected for the Naval Examination Service during the Great War. Had the Captain served? But no, how foolish of him, the Captain was too young.

Stanier listened as patiently as he could while Jones conducted him round the various files and boxes that constituted the Harbour Master's office. Eventually the coxswain's loquacity died away and Stanier spoke for the first time.

Pulling his watch from his waistcoat he said, 'Thank you, Mr Jones. I see it wants but ten minutes to high water; would you be kind enough to tell me what movements we have?'

Jones waved his hand airily towards the harbour entrance. 'Fred and Stan have the c'soons open now, the fishin' boats are already out an' there goes the *Carry* ...'

For the first time since entering the building Stanier looked out. A spinney of gaily painted masts was visible round the end of the sea wall where the departing fishing boats puttered out of the harbour. One or two were already hoisting sail, each skipper's course slightly divergent from the next as they headed for their own favourite grounds.

Stanier was next aware of the dominating bulk of the *Caryatid*. The high tide caused her to tower over the granite quay and though only a small ship, in a tiny harbour like Porth Ardur her hull was imposing.

Her black top sides were badly rusted below her anchor boxes and half-way along her well-deck, where four or five brightly painted buoys sat. Seamen were busy lashing them down. Stanier, for all his experience, had never seen a ship like her before.

'What ship did you say that was?'

'The *Carry*, Cap'n, *Caryatid* properly, see. She grosses nine hundred tons and lies weekends on the lighthouse pier.'

Stanier thought fast. Nine hundred made a tidy packet in dues and she was obviously a buoy tender here in his harbour.

'What amount of dues does she pay, Mr Jones?'

'Why bless you, none, Cap'n, she's a lighthouse tender an' exempt.' Jones chuckled to himself as if he found the idea of Captain Macready paying dues vastly amusing. Stanier was annoyed with himself for betraying his ignorance.

'Ah, yes, I was forgetting, Section 357 of the Merchant Shipping Act. So she works out of Porth Ardur ...'

'Port' Ardur, Cap'n ...'

'Pardon?'

'It's "Port", you don't sound the "h" but pass quickly to the name, so you sort of run the two together.'

'I see,' said Stanier, colouring.

Jones ignored the Captain's discomfiture. 'Aye, she runs out of 'ere most weeks, just occasionally she's away over a weekend, then you'll get all the wives and sweet'earts coming down for news. Drives a man bloody crazy. Sometimes she goes out at weekends for emergency calls but not often. Captain Macready tries to avoid it as most of the crew either fail to muster or are too drunk to be much use.'

'I see. That's Captain Macready up on the bridge, is it?' Jones looked up.

'That's 'im, Cap'n. They call him "Ebb-Tide Macready" as 'e's always going out.' Jones chuckled again and quietly noted the humour was lost on Stanier. Odd, he thought, how a man could have education and no sense of humour. Stanier was looking up at the portly bulk of Macready, arrogantly self-confident, the gold braid at his cuffs flashing in the sunlight as he rang

40

the engine room telegraphs.

'My God, he looks like the Master of the *Mauretania!*'

Jones laughed again. 'Oh, they run them lighthouse tenders really tiddly like. You wait 'til the Commissioners come, Cap'n. Oh, she's a smart little ship an' no mistake.'

'Does she tend our buoys?'

Jones nodded. 'We've two in the bay she renews 'em ev'ry year. You have to pay rent for 'em, about three pounds I think it is.'

'Rent? But surely we have jurisdiction over the *Caryatid?*' Stanier looked surprised.

Jones suppressed another laugh. 'Oh no Cap'n, nobody has jurisdiction over old "Ebb Tide", excep' the Commissioners— and as they only come once a year ...' He shrugged and tailed off, further explanation seemed superfluous.

Stanier was beginning to dislike Captain Macready. In his miserable brick hut he was beginning to feel that the real kingdom of his harbour had been usurped by another. 'What about my predecessor? How did he get on with, er, *Captain* Macready?'

'Oh, very well, sir. They were close friends. You don't want to worry, Captain Stanier. Just treat the old *Caryatid* as a matter of routine.'

Bernard Foster took over the bridge from Captain Macready before *Caryatid* was clear of the bay. Macready went below and summoned his new Second Mate. Charlie was charmed both by the Captain, whose attitude was avuncular, and by his cabin which was richly panelled, with bright chintz curtains looped about polished brass ports. The twin barrels of a matching clock and barometer were secured to the bulkhead above the diminutive knee-hole desk. Beyond, Charlie sensed rather than saw the Captain's tiny night cabin.

'Well Mr, er, Farthing, so you've decided to join the Lighthouse Service?'

Charlie nodded. 'Yessir.'

Macready looked hard at the young man. He was thin, yet his wrists seemed sinewy enough. The grey eyes met his own coolly, the tall body swaying as the steamer met the first of the Atlantic swells rolling in from the open sea. Macready questioned the new officer as to his past experience.

'Mate's Ticket, sir. Most of my time in cargo ships, a little in coasters including two passages in ketches.'

'D'you get on all right in small boats?'

'Yes, sir.'

'Good. Now if you go up to the bridge Mr Foster will outline your routine duties and explain the broader points of our job. You can't expect to learn it in a day, there's *no* teacher like experience ... right, thank you Mr, er, Farthing ...'

Up on the bridge Charlie found the ship had cleared the bay completely. The headland that guarded the approaches to Porth Ardur was falling astern, a huge jagged escarpment of fissured rock that seemed to jut out into the sea like a vast fist.

The fresh southwesterly breeze had set up a choppy sea that opposed the ebb tide now sweeping the *Caryatid* westwards. Ahead on the port bow, blue with distance, Charlie could just make out the hump-backed outline of an island. Foster took him into the chartroom. Picking out a general chart of the area the Mate described the area tended by the old steamer.

'This is our principal operational area,' began Foster, tapping the chart with a pair of brass dividers. 'The Channel is about eighty miles long. The main commercial port is at the narrow eastern end here.' He tapped a spot that Charlie recognised as the junction through which he had passed that morning. 'The south shore is mainly steep-to, though with many off-lying dangers.' Foster indicated buoys marking rocks and banks. 'The north shore is more complex. There are coal exporting ports here and here.' Charlie remembered the pithead gear. 'There is a lower coast further to the west, plenty of agricultural land which slopes into the sea and produces a large area of sand banks and bars which we mark, but only local fishermen use. Then the country becomes more mountainous again with our base there at Porth Ardur and only small fishing ports to the west where the coast swings away north again. There's a regular archipelago off these headlands and we supply two lighthouses there. The main channel is pretty deep. The main offshore danger is the Hellweather Bank marked by buoys and a lightvessel. Then further down to the west the island of Ynyscraven, that's it fine to port, we're bound there now, that's got a lighthouse, and further west still is the isolated rock station known as Buccabu lighthouse.'

'And it's our job to maintain all the buoys and supply the lightvessel and the lighthouses?'

'That's about it. There are the four principal lighthouses and the Hellweather lightvessel, a number of lesser lighthouses, most actually unwatched beacons, four granite daymarks we land and paint annually and eighty buoys, some lit, some not.'

Charlie nodded. Foster went on to tell Charlie of his duties aboard and explained the procedure for landing. 'I'll come with you to Ynyscraven today and show you the

45

ropes. After that you'll be on your own, though the boat's crew'll help, alright?'

'I think so, Mr Foster.'

Foster lit his pipe. 'Call me Bernard, for heaven's sake, reserve the "sirs" for the old man.'

'What's he like?' enquired Charlie, adding hurriedly, 'He seemed pleasant enough to me.'

Foster puffed ruminatively on his pipe for a minute, then he said, 'You'll not find a better seaman anywhere but don't emphasise your foreign exploits too much. What certificate've you got?'

'First Mate's,' replied Charlie. Foster nodded. 'Good, I've a Master's but I like a quiet life and I don't much talk about it, or how I got it. I'd advise you to do the same.'

'I'm sorry Mr, er, Bernard, I don't think I quite understand.'

Foster drew again on his pipe and moved away onto the open bridge out of earshot of the man at the wheel. He motioned Charlie to follow him.

'Captain Macready joined the Service

as a boy. He's had no qualifying time for Board of Trade certificates but in the old days Lighthouse Service officers were self-examining. The Masters sat on a board with one of the Commissioners and set exams for the likes of you and me. They were specialist exams in our work and quite tough. But the bureaucrats don't recognise such practical things. Now we all have to have tickets like you and me. A few old-timers are left, like Macready, and many of them resent us as interlopers. So be a bit diplomatic. D'you savvy now?'

'Yes, yes of course ...' Charlie sounded a little dubious.

'Mind you,' asserted the Mate, stabbing his pipe stem in Charlie's direction, 'you won't find a finer seaman than our Septimus. I've seen him do the most fantastic things with this ship and the men love him, you wait until tonight, you'll see. Just because he doesn't have a bit of paper doesn't mean he's no sailor, and it doesn't mean he isn't Captain and Master of this ship. One or two smart-arses have made that mistake.' Foster chuckled reminiscently to himself and turned away into the wheelhouse, leaving Charlie musing on the bridge wing.

What an extraordinary day it was turning out to be. He had never thought he would stand on the bridge of a ship whose master had no qualifications. Or at least, no formal ones, he hurriedly corrected himself, mindful of the Mate's admonitions.

A patter of spray flew round the break of the fo'c's'le and streamed across the well-deck. Instantly the stays and guys were bedewed with tiny drops that gleamed in the sunshine.

Perhaps, thought Charlie, I have found fairy-land after all.

Stanier spent the remainder of the day being shown round by Mr Jones. In the main his enthusiasm waned. He was shown the *Caryatid*'s berth which was always to be kept clear. That alone seemed an infringement of his authority as the Harbour Master. Even more infuriating, when compared with his little brick caboose, was the Lighthouse Authority's compound. At the inner end of the Lighthouse Pier a stone wall enclosed a large area above which could be seen the tops of several score of buoys. They were red, green, black, chequered in various combinations and of differing shapes. There was also a store and an office building which housed the administrative staff of two old clerks and several girls and women. Outside was a flagpole from which the Authority's ensign snapped sharply in the breeze.

'Quite a set-up,' Stanier muttered more to himself than to Jones, but the latter detected the envy and chuckled quietly to himself They completed the circuit of the inner basin and walked out along the mole. At its outer end there was another flag-pole with a yard.

''Ere we 'oist the shapes and lanterns to show the port's open or closed, Cap'n Stanier. Two lanterns 'orizontal means open for outward movements, four in a square means open for inwards. Fred and Stan look after them altering them according to the c'soons. I usually tells 'em when there's enough water on the sill, unless of course you'd like to do that in future?'

Stanier looked up at the yard, swaying slightly in the wind. If he did not do that he would have very little to do except fill in forms in the brick caboose. He was suddenly angry. 'Yes! Yes, of course I'll take that responsibility. You'll do nothing about hoisting signals or moving the caisson without my instructions. Do you understand, Mr Jones?'

'Perfectly, Cap'n,' said Thomas soothingly, already preparing the rhetoric, he would use later to explain the new Harbour Master to the lads in The Feathers.

Stanier turned away then stopped, swinging abruptly round on Jones. 'And furthermore, we'll carry out a survey of the harbour approaches starting tomorrow morning ...'

By evening, however, two things had soothed Stanier's battered pride a little. The first was his launch. This was a splendid teak boat some thirty-six feet long. It was steam propelled and agleam with polished brass, miniature ventilators, and lined with scrubbed teak gratings. Every cleat and fairlead gleamed with polish and the varnish was similarly bright.

But the greater boost to his morale came as they traversed the inner harbour. This area was filled with a few rowing boats and yachts, and a larger number of open, inshore fishing boats. It was tidal and dried at low water springs. At the end was a small dry-dock which Stanier had missed earlier. A small coaster squatted on the blocks, old pit props acting as side shores to hold her ample tumblehome secure.

'This 'elps a bit of revenue into the port, Cap'n,' explained Mr Jones. 'And it does you a bit of good on the side, like.' Jones leered at the Harbour Master.

'Does it?' queried Stanier.

'Of course, Cap'n, as Harbour Master you're also pilot, both for the basin and for the dock. Can't fail to make a bit out of that, now, not to mention the odd bottle ...'

After they had returned to the abhorred

brick caboose and pored over accounts and dusty documents, from which Stanier gathered that Edwardes had been as lax over his paperwork as over the correct procedures to be adopted when running a port, Jones suggested a drink. It was just after six when the two men entered The Feathers. Stanier had only intended to have a sociable drink with his underling and then return to his hotel, or to be correct, Porth Ardur's only hotel. However, about half an hour after his arrival another person came in. Tegwyn Morgan, eighteen-year-old daughter of Justine, slipped behind the bar and in sliding out of her coat destroyed Stanier's hitherto impeccable self-possession.

Having spent the succeeding hour contemplating her body as she bent to oblige successive customers, he realised he was succumbing to lust as much as to alcohol. In a wave of self-revelation he made his apologies, thanked Mr Jones for his time and wove, with as much dignity as his twenty-six years could muster, his way out.

Straightening up and smoothing her dress over her hips, Tegwyn smiled at Mr Jones. 'Who's your new friend, Tom love?'

'That, my dear, is the new 'Arbour Master. Captain bloody Stanier.'

'He's young, isn't he; quite good looking too.'

Avalon

If, in the last hours of Sunday, Charlie
Farthing had idly ruminated on the
possibility of discovering a land of enchantment somewhere west of the railway
terminus, by the early hours of Tuesday
he was almost certain. His certainty was
incomplete for by this time, although
delighted with the situation he found
himself in, his breast was racked by
emotions more immediate and desperately
assertive than the simple realisation that
he, as an animal, had stumbled upon the
perfect habitat.

The *Caryatid* let go her anchor in
fifteen fathoms off the north-east corner
off Ynyscraven at about four in the
afternoon. The breeze was dropping but
the sea was still lively. It was already past
low water but the flood was yet young and
the rocky, grey cliffs showed exposed and

54

shiny lower slopes where slime and weed marked the full tidal range. Ynyscraven's northern tip bore the white lighthouse that *Caryatid* had come to service. It was situated below the highest point of the island, precariously balanced upon a shelf of rock from which the cliffs dropped away in broken, creviced rock, old as time and inhabited by little tufts of thrift and a million sea birds. Kittiwakes, fulmars, razorbills and guillemots were the most numerous, but here and there squat little puffins, with their bright coloured beaks and their web feet trailing like hastily stowed under carriages, whirled their rapid wing beats across the sea. The air was alive with the screams of the birds but Charlie's thoughts were broken into by the Captain. Macready had been studying the foot of the cliffs through binoculars. Alongside him Foster was doing the same.

'About four foot lift,' Foster muttered helpfully.

'Yes, I think as you're going in it'll be alright. Anyway, see how it goes.'

The Mate turned to Charlie. 'Come on,

we'll show you what this is all about.' Charlie followed Foster down the bridge ladder and along the boat deck. With a deceptively casual activity one of *Caryatid*'s boats was being prepared.

A few minutes later Charlie found himself bobbing over the sea, the motor boat lifting effortlessly over the ground swell and flinging aside spray from the wind sea. Tidal eddies further complicated the wave patterns so that the boat seemed like an ancient war canoe picking its way between Scylla and Charybdis. This illusion was heightened by the black rocks that rose on either side of them as they approached the landing. To one of these massive outcrops was secured the end of a wire.

'The hoist wire for landing stores,' explained Foster. 'Boat lies underneath and signals to the winch house ...' Charlie looked up to where, perched on a rock outcrop, a little cement hut stood next to a gantry over which the other end of the wire ran. He nodded. Ahead of them the cliff shut out sunlight and they motored into a cool gloom. All around the suck and whirl of the swells lifted and dropped them as though they were gliding over the back of some vast, sub-aquaeous monster that respirated gently beneath them. The landing was in sight and in a sudden bemusing flurry of activity a stern anchor had been pitched over the boat's stern, its hemp rope smoking over an oak king-post. White water was all around them and Charlie's heart beat suddenly faster. He was aware too that the boat's crew now worked with a concentrated energy, though scarcely a word was passed between them. A heaving line snaked through the air and was quickly caught. Charlie could see two keepers above him on a granite platform from which steps vanished up the towering cliff above and behind them. Another line came aboard, there was the rattle of chain where the boat ropes ended in chain snotters to prevent chafe on the rocks and suddenly the boat was secured, surging forwards and backwards, rising and falling, held by the snapping ropes that confined her like a fractious horse. Foster,

Charlie and the working party leapt ashore and began the long, breathtaking climb up the steps.

The next two hours proved utterly fascinating. The boat returned to *Caryatid* and ran successive loads of oil barrels in under the hoist wire from where they were winched aloft. Once the seamen had started work Foster took Charlie off to see the lighthouse. They strode through the immaculately kept quarters and ascended the lantern tower. Foster showed Charlie the enormous optic and demonstrated how easily it was turned by an overgrown clockwork motor. At the centre of the foci the paraffin vapour burner sat, an innocent-looking apparatus of great importance and reliability. With something akin to a shock Charlie realised how he, in common with most seamen, took the wink of a lighthouse so utterly for granted.

'It's most interesting, Bernard,' said Charlie as they came back out into the daylight. 'How often do we bring oil and water?'

'We don't need to bring water very

often, the lighthouse has a flat roof over the dwellings to act as a catchment. We deliver oil about once a quarter.'

'One other thing, I noticed the lantern level was well below the highest point of the island ... that seems a bit odd to me ...'

The Mate nodded. 'They built the first tower on the highest point but found that ten months out of twelve it was in cloud. This one's just below the level of normal orographic cloud and has a range of twenty-four miles in all but fog or very heavy precipitation.'

They began the long descent to the boat. Around them the sea birds whirled and screamed. 'They're nesting,' explained Foster. Tufts of thrift, moss, fern and heather gave way to lichens as they descended and at the foot of the cliff they waited once more. The smell of ozone was invigorating in Charlie's nostrils and he inhaled it enthusiastically. He watched the boat come in, impressed with the confidence with which the coxswain relied upon the keepers, though equally careful of his stern anchor line as his only escape should a swell pick up the boat and surge it forward. There was only sheer rock ahead and Charlie was beginning to appreciate some of that 'experience' Macready and Foster had been emphasising.

They returned through the swirling waters; the tide was much higher now. On several isolated pinnacles of rock cormorants and the greener crested shags sat drying their wings. They looked like Teutonic eagles atop pointed helmets. Charlie smiled to himself. He liked the imagery. They were the helmets of giant warriors hurled from the cliff-top by some Arthurian vedette long ago.

Charlie had one last surprise. As the launch rounded *Caryatid*'s stern he looked up. The steamer's stern was in considerable contrast to her workmanlike bow. A counter that would have graced a sailing ship extended out over the rudder post. Knuckled twice it bore a handsomely carved set of trail boards painted in gilt, red, green and blue. A scroll work of seaweeds and fishes terminated in naked females who bore flaming cressets and between these two devices, one on either quarter, was the name *Caryatid* and her port of registry. Foster saw his fascination. 'It's poetic licence really,' he offered by way of explanation. 'Caryatids are supposed to bear up the roofs of temples but ...' he shrugged, 'the idea of supporting, in their case, seamarks is quite apt ...'

Charlie nodded. The next minute they were alongside and hooking on. Seconds later, with a clatter of the steam winch and a creaking of manila falls, the launch was being hoisted into the davits.

The *Caryatid* was brought to an anchor for the night some three miles south of the lighthouse off the southern end of Ynyscraven. As was his custom Captain Macready announced to his officers after dinner that the off duty watch could have a run ashore. Charlie, who had no idea whether or not he was on or off duty when at anchor, enquired of the Mate. Bernard Foster puffed his pipe, a twinkle in his eye. 'Strictly speaking it's your turn, the port watch being off tonight, but I think you'll benefit more from a run ashore. I'm not bothered about going and the Chief and I'll have a game of cribbage. You go off and gather some local colour.'

It was already dusk when the motor launch left *Caryatid*'s side. The last man into the boat had been Calico Jack who had slid down the man-ropes to the jeers of his fellows waiting thirstily in the well of the boat. Somewhat impatiently Charlie watched the boat go. He had been told by the Mate to wait for Captain Macready. When the boat returned Charlie slid into it and waited. A few minutes later the portly backside of his commander swung into view. Half suspended, the Captain exchanged a few words with Foster then descended into the launch.

The boat turned away from the ship and approached the island some three and a half cables distant. Macready stared appraisingly at *Caryatid* then abruptly turned and viewed the land.

Ynyscraven lay like some enormous dragon. The lighthouse was situated on its north point, where the dragon's head might be imagined to lie. The greater, higher part of the island, little better than heather-covered moor, formed the beast's back, gradually sloping away to a slightly lower plateau.

As if reading Charlie's thoughts the Captain said, 'Beautiful spot, Mr Farthing.'

'Yes it is sir, I was just thinking the same.'

'There's a bit of farming done this end,' he waved to the south where a few low houses could be seen by their lights. 'Mostly sheep, although they domesticate the wild ponies for a living.'

'Much of a population, sir?'

The Captain shook his head. 'No. There's the owner's reeve, two or three shepherd families and a couple of crack-pots. In the summer you get the visiting ornithologists, probably a few there now since the birds are breeding.'

The boat slowed and came alongside a low stone jetty. The Captain and Charlie jumped ashore. They were in the shadow of a steep hill and in almost total darkness.

'There's the path, you go on ahead, I just want a word with the coxswain.'

Charlie started off. He had a sudden desire to be on his own and began to walk briskly upwards. Gorse and bracken spurted out of little hollows in the rock but everywhere granite outcrops predominated. The path led up the side of a small valley. Below him to his right Charlie could hear a little stream and he could see where denser and more luxuriant vegetation grew. The air was scented with damp, pleasant odours and he continued upwards for several minutes without any sound of the Captain behind him. He failed to notice a fork in the path where it crossed the head of the valley. A fairly large stone house stood in a little coombe. He continued climbing, the path winding round behind the house. Ahead of him he could see open sky, and realised he was reaching the summit of the island. Just before he emerged from the vegetation onto rough pasture the figure of a girl stepped out in front of him. The encounter was abrupt, with the quality of ambuscade about it.

'Hullo,' she said. He could barely make out her features since she was silhouetted against what daylight remained in the western sky, but her voice was low and self-confident.

'Oh, hullo,' he replied, taken aback.

'Did I startle you?' There was a note of mockery in her voice.

'A little,' he replied.

'Only you're going the wrong way ... to the pub that is.'

'Am I? Oh, I'm sorry. I didn't really know that's where I was supposed to be going.'

'You *are* off the *Caryatid?*' she asked suspiciously.

'Yes,' he replied.

'Well,' she said firmly, 'the *Caryatid*'s people always go to the pub.' There was such an emphasis on 'always' that Charlie began to assume he was trespassing.

'I beg your pardon, I was really just walking, following the path, I didn't know I was trespassing.'

She laughed, a light refreshing laugh. 'You're not,' she said reassuringly, 'it's just unusual to see one of *Caryatid*'s crew not on the pub path. I expected you to take the path to the right of the reeve's house, it runs alongside his garden, you go through the old monastery wall and the pub-cum-post office is right there.'

'Oh, I see.' He pondered a minute. 'What did you mean when you said you "expected"?'

She laughed again. 'Oh, I was watching you and Mr Foster up at the lighthouse this afternoon ... through my glasses from the crags above the hoist gantry.'

Charlie vaguely remembered some huge rock outcrops behind and above the little lighthouse plateau.

'Then you have the advantage over me. Name's Charlie Farthing. I've just joined the *Caryatid* as Second Mate. This morning as a matter of fact.'

He held out his hand feeling rather foolish since they could now hardly see each other. He was instantly hurt when she ignored it. A note of asperity came into her voice: 'What do you think of Ynyscraven?' she asked. For a minute he was tempted to reply, 'not much,' since the manners of the inhabitants left much to be desired but there was that hint of interrogation in the question that made him think he was being tested.

'I think it the most beautiful place I have ever seen,' he said without falsehood. 'Now will you tell me who you are and shake my hand or are you really a sprite about to disappear?'

His intuition had been correct but the girl's response exceeded his expectations. She grasped his outstretched hand, suddenly leant forward and brushed her lips against his cheek. Then, still holding his hand, she pulled away laughing. 'Come *on* then, I've been waiting ages for you.'

In the next hour and a half Charlie lost his heart. He was comfortably euphoric after a poor night's sleep and the exertions of the day. The girl took him across the spine of the island to the cliff-tops of the western side. At this point Ynyscraven was only three hundred yards wide and the walk across a springy turf being cropped by the ghostly forms of sheep seemed to him to take but a few seconds. They sat down below the sky line.

To left and right of them the broken, precipitous cliffs of the island stretched away. Far below the restless Atlantic pounded at their feet, a white filigree of foam lacing the shore. The westerly wind was deflected upwards so that here they were in total peace, above them the pale shapes of ridge-soaring gulls screamed into the night. Before them the infinite vista of the dark ocean and the vast canopy of sky as the planet plunged into night seemed quite personal to them.

'Quite the most beautiful place I have ever seen ...' muttered Charlie.

The girl hugged her knees then turned her head towards him.

'And have you seen many places, Mr Farthing?' she enquired mockingly.

He shrugged. 'Bits of four continents, but always as, well, a visitor.'

'But you are a visitor here.'

Charlie shook his head. 'I am to you. But as a sailor that,' he indicated the ocean below them, inky blue in the night, 'that is my home until I choose somewhere to swallow the anchor. Besides, I'm a bit of the *Caryatid* and she seems to be part of the seascape hereabouts.'

He heard her chuckle softly in the darkness.

'Tell me why is this island *so* important to you?' he asked, sensing rather than seeing her shrug.

'I was born here. Perhaps I was taught as a little girl to dislike the outside world. I am told many people of my age wish to leave the places they are born in but I have no wish to leave this place. Ever!' Her voice, which began dreamily, ended emphatically, as though warning Charlie. It made him think of an earlier remark.

'And why did you say you had been waiting ages for me?'

'You ask too many questions, Mr Farthing.' She was laughing at him again.

'But I want to. I don't even know your name. Is it Guinevere or Morgan le Fay?'

69

She rounded on him sharply. 'Why did you say that?' The sharp, interrogative, even imperious note was in her voice again. He told her. He told her of his wry fancy that had started the previous night at the railway station and had persisted as the train had brought him nearer and nearer to Porth Ardur. He told her how no single incident that had occurred during the day had destroyed the feeling that he was approaching a land of magic and the conviction he had felt when seeing the jettisoned helmets of the defeated warriors. He ended feeling the merest pinprick of cynical self-ridicule. Her reply laid his wandering heart at rest. Quietly she said:

'That, Charlie, is why I said I had been waiting for you.'

Very slowly she rolled over him. They kissed cautiously, not wanting to break the magic of the night with the dross of physical contact but as their lips met they both knew that a passion existed within them that seemed bottomless. After a little she drew away from him and rose to her knees. The next minute she was pulling him protesting to his feet. 'Come on,' she said, 'we must go to the pub. They'll be missing you by now and when they find you they'll accuse you of doing unspeakable things with sheep.'

Charlie roared with laughter. It was an accurate assessment. 'Hold on a minute,' he pulled her back. 'I still don't know your name.'

'It's Sonia,' she said daring him to laugh. 'It's Slavic, you know, now *come on!*'

The public house which went under the grandiloquent title of the Craven Arms was a large, open, stone hall. It had a wooden bar along one side and barrels of spigoted beer on cradles. Three small kegs of spirits were similarly rigged and the walls were decorated with the nautical paraphernalia which has since become so popular but which was, in the case of the Craven Arms, entirely plundered or washed ashore from wrecks. In the sense of being a public place the Craven Arms fulfilled its function admirably. When the *Caryatid* anchored the little island usually went *en fête*. Almost its entire population was present. The atmosphere was thick with smoke, loud chatter and the clink of glasses. The oil lamps caught the sheen of perspiration on rosy faces and the slopping amber of beer in glasses. The atmosphere was decidedly convivial.

When Charlie and the girl arrived they were greeted with cheers which Charlie found embarrassing, as much for Sonia as himself but looking at her, as she shoved her way to the bar and returned with two pints of beer, he realised she was quite used to it. He was able to see her clearly for the first time. Like himself she wore wellington boots. A pair of slacks were mostly covered by an Aran sweater. At her throat a knotted kerchief of emerald green was the only item of personal decoration she wore. Her features were regular and broad, her hair was reddish, neither auburn nor carroty, and a pair of level green eyes looked at him from beneath arched brows. On each slightly prominent cheekbone her creamy skin was slightly wind-burned and freckled.

'Disappointed?' she asked handing him a glass of beer.

'I don't answer *that*,' he laughed, 'and you?'

'You forget I've been watching you this afternoon.'

Charlie rubbed a bristly chin, wondering what on earth she saw in his unremarkable features. He shrugged. 'Good,' he said and they smiled at each other.

This intimate conversation was carried out at a shout whilst the two lovers were being gently jostled by the other inhabitants of the bar. These were well on the way to intoxication and Charlie looked round for Macready. The Captain, still in his brass-bound reefer sat in a corner. Before him were a large glass of brandy and his hat. With him sat a tall, florid man and they were in conversation. There was a tiny, yet distinct, gap around them as though the company acknowledged the social difference of the two gentlemen, conceded them a trifling privacy before proceeding with its own merriment.

'Your Captain's talking to the reeve. He's

the agent of the owner. The island belongs to the estate of the Earl of Dungarth. I believe Mr Hamilton was his adjutant in the war. He and old "Ebb Tide" always chinwag like that.'

An accordion started up. Mackerel Jack began to play a reel and there was a move to dance. A little space was cleared at the end of the bar and two of the locals and their women spun into the ring. Next was Calico Jack, jerking energetically around an odd little woman to the cheers of his shipmates. The woman wore a fur coat that had seen better days. She appeared not to notice the sweltering heat in the place, though her grey hair hung in wispy disorder about her head.

'Who on earth is that little old woman?' Charlie asked Sonia.

'That's Mother. Come on, we'll dance now!' Charlie's surprise had not turned to protest before he found himself whirling alongside the old woman. Calico Jack's happily inebriated face came and went around the bulk of her fur coat like an alcoholic moon as *Caryatid*'s crew pounded out the rhythm nodding and smiling to each other that their new Second Mate seemed a good lad and a sport and a lucky bastard to have got the daughter.

'Give 'em a fuckin' waltz, Mack,' yelled one of the greasers and Mackerel Jack, to the accompaniment of knowing leers and winks, slowed down the music so that all the gyrating partners lost their timing then melted into linked couples. Calico Jack disappeared into the vast fur coat, the shepherds grabbed their women tightly, possessively, with so many seamen in the room. One off duty lighthouse keeper held his affianced shepherdess with a discreet tenderness and two seamen, who had been dancing an improvised hornpipe between them said, 'Oh, fuck it!' and sat down, grinning into their beer.

Mackerel excelled himself, slowing the waltz down to a melancholic chanty tune that the men hummed. Some of them had sat in the horse latitudes on the decks of windjammers humming the tune of 'Leave her Johnnie' as their vessels idly rolled in the calm; all of them were affected by it and all watched the dancing couples without ridicule.

Charlie was lost in the perfume of Sonia's hair; feeling her thighs against his he gently pushed his pelvis forward and was met by an answering thrust. He felt her breasts against his chest and leaned his body closer to hers, trying to keep the revelation of his own arousal private between them. As the music slowed to its end he kissed her, briefly but publicly. There was a moment of silence, then a storm of shouts and cheering. Glasses were banged on the table and booted feet stamped on the granite flags of the floor.

Mackerel swung into another jig and the locals relinquished their women as the Caryatids swept into the next dance. Somebody pulled Calico Jack out of his furry burrow and demanded he bought the next round.

Sonia pulled Charlie back to the bar. 'It's your turn too,' she said. They were laughing at each other like children. While he stood at the slopped wood surface he looked about him. 'It's like a Viking hall,' he said. She nodded.

'Or Camelot?' he went on. She frowned and shook her head.

'No,' she replied seriously, 'no, Camelot was corrupted, this is Avalon.'

They clicked glasses, laughing again.

Charlie looked several times at the old woman Sonia had described as her mother. She was sitting quietly with Calico Jack, taking no part in the conversation of the fireman and his mates but staring ahead of her. He turned to the girl.

'Your mother, is she alright?' Sonia looked quickly at her mother and nodded.

'She's alright. I'll explain one day.'

Charlie was going to press her but someone was up and singing now. It was a popular and sugary ballad that evoked enthusiastic applause. Other songs followed in which the company joined or talked through, according to inclination. At last Mackerel Jack played an obviously familiar chanty. Charlie was beginning to join in when he felt the girl's hand on his arm. 'You'll be going soon, they always play the chanties when the Captain tells them.

Everyone knows it's time to go ...' She trailed off. He bent and kissed her, feeling someone behind him slopping beer down his back. 'Will I see you again?' he asked, wondering if he was being played with in a manner he was not unacquainted with.

'Of course,' she breathed at him; then she looked away and, in a clear, strong voice, joined in the chanty. Charlie could have sworn afterwards that there were tears in her eyes.

They sang 'The Hog's Eye Man' and the 'Arethusa' then broke into 'Spanish Ladies'. At the last verse, 'Now let every man fill up his full bumper ...' glasses were drained for the last time. The chanty, old when Nelson was a midshipman, finished in cheers which gradually died away. Sonia nudged him and nodded in Captain Macready's direction. Macready had risen and made a great show of looking at his watch. 'God bless my soul, it's midnight,' he intoned and from the assembled grins Charlie guessed it was a ritual. The Captain looked up. 'Mackerel!' he said sharply.

'Sir?' mocked the able seaman back.

'My song, please.' If Charlie had expected some ghastly piece of self-aggrandisement he was pleasantly disappointed. In a remarkably fine baritone Septimus Macready launched into the most plaintive of all sea chanties:

'Oh Shenandoah I long to see you,
Away you rolling river,
Oh Shenandoah I long to hold you,
And away, we're bound away 'cross the
     wide Missouri ...'

Charlie found himself clutching Sonia's waist as the whole company swayed gently to the haunting tune. There was no applause at the end of the song. The Captain paused a second to swallow, jammed his cap on and, waving to the barman flung open the door and strode into the night. His alcohol-bemused and happy crew followed him, trailing out into the moon-flooded night.

Sonia held Charlie's hand while they followed the file of men. They passed through the old monastery wall and descended the path by which Charlie should have come up earlier. In the

moonlight Charlie recognised the bifur-
cation and here Sonia said goodnight.
They clung together for a long while.
He longed to squeeze her breasts but
had an intuitively repressive thought not
to sharpen his desire further. At last
they drew apart. 'Good night, Charlie
darling,' she whispered and turning away
into the undergrowth she disappeared. For
a minute he stood there in the moonlight.
Was it the same moon he had seen
rising over the capital's jumbled roofs
and chimneys? He shook off the thought
and turned away, hurrying down after the
retreating crew.

He caught them up as they tumbled
into the boat. Aft with the cox he saw
Captain Macready. 'Mr Farthing!' the
Captain called.

'Sir?'

'Officers aft, if you please.' With much
scrambling Charlie pushed aft. The men
drew good-naturedly aside, not interrupting
their conversation as he passed.

'D'you hear what Calico says there,
Harry boy-o?'

'Whash tha'?'

'The old 'un. Under that mountain of fur she was naked ...'

'Cor fuck me ...'

A Disagreement

Captain James St John Stanier, Harbour Master of Porth Ardur, had by the middle of his first week in his new job, got his feet well under the table. Having insisted 'his staff' kept him fully informed and made no moves to berth, shift or unmoor ships without his express permission, he was to be seen strutting about the quay side at tide time full, as Thomas Jones told the lads in The Feathers 'of piss and importance.'

Thomas, Fred and Stan were convinced the new broom would soon get tired of its clean sweeping and went along with their new governor's ways. All of them sensed a change in the weather and anticipated the passenger-ship trained 'Captain' would not favour dirty weather half so much.

Unaware that he was also the butt of jokes amongst the fishermen, Stanier pressed on regardless of the sly glances and smirks he engendered. On Tuesday afternoon one of the *schuyts* sailed. The skipper sent for a pilot and Stanier duly went aboard. The Dutch skipper took no notice of Stanier and seemed content that the pilot was simply there. With a massive paw on the wheel, another on the engine room telegraph (which he appeared to be about to break with every swing) and a string of roared commands at his mate on the fo'c's'le, the Dutchman got his coaster warped across the basin. Once lined up with the entrance he slammed the telegraph full ahead and the *schuyt* steamed straight through the lockheads, swung round the end of the mole and slowed to disembark the pilot. Leaving the wheel the Dutchman proffered a paw to Stanier. 'Dank you, pilot.' They shook hands, Stanier took his signed chit and the Dutchman disappeared into his wheelhouse again. Stanier beat a hasty retreat. At least his launch was a credit to him, he thought, jumping into it.

'That was as neat a piece of ship handling

as I've seen, Captain,' said Jones innocently when Stanier sat beside him. 'Yes, thank you,' replied Stanier, his blush told Jones what the latter already suspected.

Despite this blow to his pride, Stanier soon forgot it as he made progress on another front. In coming to Porth Ardur it was not his intention to become romantically entangled. His one intention was to enhance his career. However, as a junior officer in a passenger-liner his life had encompassed a fair amount of sexual activity. It was therefore logical that he should seek a compliant and discreet bed-partner with whom he could establish a casual relationship. Although his experience in such matters was not inconsiderable his assumptions about the female sex were apt to be naively based upon the atmosphere on board passenger-liners sailing under sexually awakening tropical skies. The metamorphoses experienced by women in such circumstances were unlikely to occur on the home ground of Porth Ardur, even given the handsome features of James St John Stanier.

On the other hand the sailor was himself susceptible to certain females. He had stared with shameless candour at Tegwyn Morgan because she had walked into his life and fulfilled his ultimate dreams of sexual fantasy. As he had striven to do his duty by the shipping company with matrons approaching the autumn of their lives he had improved his performance with a little harmless (and encouraging) day-dreaming. Tegwyn Morgan exactly fitted his image of a *femme fatale* and Captain Stanier took to drinking in The Feathers regularly.

It was not until Thursday night that Stanier also met Justine. She was pleasant chatty and, discovering that Stanier was a dancer, invited him to the dancing group's club night the following evening.

'Does your daughter dance as well?' Stanier asked, too casually to fool Justine. She shrugged, 'Occasionally, when she's in the mood.'

She laughed, a rich bubbling laugh so that Stanier looked from mother to daughter and licked his lips. He did not notice further along the bar several elderly men apparently abstractedly supping pints. Their concentration was riveted on Stanier.

Tide time on Friday was 1148. Punctually at 1130 *Caryatid* appeared in the bay. The weather had turned. After leaving Ynyscraven the ship had steamed west southwest to where the Buccabu Reef rose from the bed of the Atlantic. The eroded residue of a once mighty escarpment, it was barely covered at high water and on its largest rock summit human ingenuity had eventually succeeded in erecting a tower lighthouse.

The Buccabu lighthouse consisted of nearly 6,000 tons of fully interlocking granite blocks, from the summit of which a mighty optic shot out the beams of light that it collected from the paraffin vapour burner at its focus. It had no adjacent dwellings, rising like the bole of an oak tree to its immense height of 139 feet above high water. Charlie had been terrified and then impressed at the expedition with which his boat's crew had removed one of the keepers. Slinging over the stern anchor he had seen them use at Ynyscraven, the boat had run in with the swell under it. At a shout from the coxswain the line had been checked. The keepers on the set-off tossed their heavy lines and, as if by magic, the boat was suddenly secured by two head ropes. If the stern anchor dragged the swell would pick the boat up and ... Charlie shivered, suddenly thinking of Sonia.

An hour after *Caryatid* had recovered her boat the first rain began to fall. It swept in a grey curtain from the west, shutting in the visibility and towing a rising wind in its skirts. Charlie remembered the old doggerel:

'Comes the rain before the wind,
 Then your sheets and halyards mind.'

Within a further two hours *Caryatid* was running before a southwesterly gale. Captain Macready decided to take his ship back to Ynyscraven until the weather moderated and *Caryatid* spent nearly twenty-four hours anchored under the lee of Charlie's private Avalon. But there was no shore leave while the gale blew. Charlie was miserable for the first time, staring disconsolately ashore in the forlorn hope he might see Sonia. Further along the boat deck he was astonished to see the figure of Calico Jack similarly lovelorn. Then, late in the afternoon, he caught sight of her. A tiny figure high up, leaning against a rock, the white sweater clear against the dark stone. He picked up the long glass and trained it, steadying the telescope against a stanchion. She had her arms about her neck. She seemed to be adjusting something at her neckline. He saw her pull her green silk scarf clear of her throat and shake her hair free. Then she walked further uphill until she stood on the skyline and stood, arm upstretched, her scarf and russet hair an oriflamme against the grey backdrop of the sky.

Charlie watched her for several moments before he granted her the courtesy of a reply. Grabbing the bridge semaphore controls he set the wooden arms whirring on the monkey island above him. He spelled out 'I love you'. Behind him a voice chuckled. Spinning round he found Captain Macready regarding him with some indulgence.

'Like to be ashore, eh, Mr Farthing?'

'Er, yes sir, very much.'

'Sorry about that. You deep-sea mariners are apt to think we coastal men spend all our lives in someone's bed. Sometimes one night out here in a gale in circumstances like yours are worth thirty drinking gin in the Indian Ocean.' He smiled sadly. 'Young love, Mr Farthing is a *very* misleading emotion—' The Captain broke off as if he had already said more than he intended. Charlie looked back to the island but Sonia had gone and another rain squall was sweeping, like a final curtain, over the scene.

'Inform the Chief we'll weigh at oh-five-hundred for Porth Ardur, let Mr Foster know as well.' Charlie left the bridge and Captain Macready paced up and down until he heard the steward ring the gong for high tea.

Captain Macready relieved his First Mate as *Caryatid* steamed round the point and entered the bay. He shaped a course of north as he had done a thousand times before, the seaman at the wheel spinning the spokes effortlessly as *Caryatid*'s patent steam tiller responded to the hydraulic pressure of the telemotor.

'Steady on north, sir,' he said.

'Very good.'

The gale still blew and despite the shelter of the land a long swell rounded the point and the steamer rolled lazily as she ploughed towards the mole of Porth Ardur. Bernard Foster finished talking to the Bosun down the voice pipe and turned idly to look out of the wheelhouse windows, waiting the few minutes until he was needed on the fo'c's'le for berthing.

He noted with pleasure the orderly state of the foredeck. The ropes coiled in their appointed places, the blake stoppers curled round their securing lugs, and the spurling pipes stopped off to prevent the sea from pouring into the ship's chain hold. He looked up and something unusual caught his eye. He picked up the glasses.

'The new Harbour Master's got the signals up against us.'

Macready uttered a grunt and lifted his own binoculars. 'Well I'm damned!'

'Perhaps he's got a coaster coming out.'

'No masts moving over the mole, Bernard ...'

'You don't suppose he's boomed the gates against the swell?'

Macready shifted his binoculars. 'There's hardly any lift along the outside of the mole. Besides, it's a sou'westerly not a bloody sou'easter. No, strikes me the new broom is trying to sweep clean. This is the first time we've had this without getting notification from the Coast Guard.' Macready stepped out onto the bridge wing and rang the engine room telegraph. The bells tinkled faintly in the engine room then jangled the acknowledgement on the bridge.

'Is Mr Farthing there?' Charlie had just come on the bridge.

'Yes, sir.'

'Mr Farthing, you're a dab hand with

the semaphore, call up the mole and ask what time we can berth.' Charlie did as he was bid. He was not to know that ashore his transmission was causing a certain amount of confusion. Thomas Jones and his mates, seeing that their new boss was full of reforming zeal and refused to delegate any responsibility, acted dumb when asked if any of them could use semaphore. It was Captain Stanier, therefore, who was thus compelled to stand conspicuously on the wind-swept mole and wave the yellow and red flags, hoist by his own petard into a position that threatened to unseat both his person and his dignity.

He read *Caryatid*'s whirling semaphore arms with some difficulty. By way of reply Stanier transmitted, 'You will enter as convenient'; he was rather proud of the last long word. By way of sealing his personal authority upon the scene he followed this up with: 'Watch for my signals'.

Stanier saw the *Caryatid* swing into the wind and the anchor ball rise at her forestay. He smiled with satisfaction.

'If we wait here too long we'll miss the bloody tide,' Macready observed to the wheelhouse in general. A hissing rain squall suddenly descended upon the ship, the wind with it lashing the little ship and tearing up the water of the bay into a million white streaks. Macready swung round with sudden decision.

'Right, let's get the launch away and land that poor bloody keeper. Mr Farthing, you go in and find out what the delay is. The men'll be wanting pay and their wives will be pestering the clerks for housekeeping and God knows what if we miss the tide ...'

Charlie clambered out of the boat and gave the grinning lighthouse keeper a hand with his gear. 'Cheerio lads,' said the keeper to the boat's crew.

'Piss off, Larry boy,' said the coxswain without malice.

The keeper laughed again from the top of the steps. 'Give her one for me then,' added the bowman. The keeper turned and looked down into the boat: 'I've two months' worth of my own to get rid of first; you'll still be waiting when I've finished.' He went chuckling off down the quay.

Charlie found Captain Stanier in his brick caboose. 'Good morning,' Charlie began. 'Can you tell me how long the *Caryatid* is likely to be kept out?'

Stanier made a great show of looking up. He regarded Charlie with some hostility. As an emissary of the magnificent Captain Septimus Macready he was somewhat unprepossessing.

'Are you an officer?' Stanier asked superciliously, staring at Charlie's plain pilot jacket, blue serge trousers and sea-boots. Charlie was annoyed.

'Captain Macready isn't in the habit of sending his cook on such errands.'

Stanier went white with suppressed fury. 'I think you had better call me "sir". And I'm sorry to mistake your identity. I'm used to seeing officers in a collar and tie.' Charlie flushed with irritation. He thought his white polo-necked sweater rather dashing. Who was this bastard anyway?

'I expect you learned your seamanship

in the passengers' bunks,' he said, 'but it doesn't matter. I'm looking for the Harbour Master—'

'*I* am the Harbour Master, Mister bloody Mate, and I'll be lodging a complaint against you when your ship berths.'

'Well, Captain,' replied Charlie with heavy emphasis, 'perhaps you'll be kind enough to tell me when that will be?'

'When I signal. Now please return to your ship.'

'That was a bit strong, you know, Captain,' said Thomas Jones who had silently witnessed the entire proceedings. Stanier leaned back in his chair, perfectly composed again.

'Mr Jones, *Caryatid* is not the only ship using this port. She must wait her turn. There is the *Sea Dragon* to sail yet.'

'But she's a blooming motor yacht, she can slip out after the ebb's away.' Jones's voice rose on a note of disbelief.

'She belongs to Sir Hector Blackadder, chairman of the Cambrian Steam Navigation Company. She dry-docks on this tide and I have been personally asked to move her round into the dock at high water. When I have cleared the gates you may signal the *Caryatid* to enter. Is that clear, Mr Jones?'

'Perfectly clear, Captain. But you're asking for trouble.'

Stanier did not hear the last remark. Donning his bridge coat, resplendent with its four bars on each shoulder, and his hat, which sat at an angle popularised by Admiral Beatty, he strode purposefully into the windy day.

It was not that Captain Stanier, wearing his other hat as Porth Ardur's pilot, made a mess of moving the *Sea Dragon*. In fact he manoeuvred strictly in accordance with the recommendations of the Board of Trade for turning vessels in a confined space. He laced the inner harbour with warps until it resembled a spider's web and gently hove the *Sea Dragon* round until her bows were in line with the gates, then he steamed gently ahead and not one inch of the yacht's paintwork was scratched. This time there was no master to interfere, since that worthy had not then been appointed.

Neither was Sir Hector in attendance, so Stanier felt his responsibility keenly.

It is true that some damage was done to the cross trees of the trawler *Cheerful Boys* but it was only the mizen mast and her owner was neither a shipping magnate nor a knight of the realm. When the little dock tug, really no more than a motor boat, came and got hold of the *Sea Dragon*'s bows and tugged her across the inner harbour to the dry-dock gates, Stanier felt his pride restored. This feeling was augmented when he saw at the door of The Feathers the voluptuous form of Tegwyn Morgan.

The main problem caused by Stanier that morning was that by the time Thomas Jones signalled the port clear for *Caryatid* to enter, the ebb was away. It was a spring tide and within an hour and a half of high water there would not be enough depth for the lighthouse tender to get over the sill.

Caryatid might have made it if she had not fouled an old trawl wire with the anchor that Stanier had made her let go by the delay. So it was thus that the *Caryatid* was compelled to remain at anchor until the next high water, around 0100 on Saturday.

It was not the first time it had happened. Occasionally the gates were boomed against a southeasterly gale, sometimes the opening mechanism failed to work, but under any circumstances it was a bitter blow to the crew of the *Caryatid*. Accustomed to arduous labour, they held their weekends sacrosanct, to be interrupted only in emergencies. For Captain Macready it was a dilemma. He would be entitled to go ashore until tide time, but scarcely felt the effort involved in a wet boat passage worthwhile. But it was Friday night and his night for dancing with Justine Morgan.

At seven o'clock *Caryatid*'s boat left the ship with half the crew. Foster watched them go. Anthea would not be pleased, but with the Captain ashore and a new second mate he felt he ought to stay. Perhaps he had an exaggerated sense of responsibility, or was it that he felt himself indispensible? He shrugged resignedly. It was just too bloody bad. He turned for his cabin and the log book.

Charlie was quite glad to stay on board. He walked quietly round *Caryatid* after the empty boat had been hoisted. The ship lifted easily to the swell that rolled into the bay. His hair was tousled by the near gale. It was definitely moderating, he thought to himself. Aft, leaning on the teak taffrail that ran round *Caryatid*'s elegant counter with the ensign cracking and snapping above him, he looked to windward. Somewhere just over the horizon, upon the island of Ynyscraven, was that strange wild creature that he was hopelessly in love with. Half-Celt, half-Slav, a combination so extraordinary that he had never heard of it before. But then he recollected that he had never been in love like this before, so perhaps it was not so very extraordinary. It was rather nice to discover a new, fresh sensation in a world which one had grown blasé about. He too shrugged and strode forward to the monastic isolation of his tiny cabin.

Justine Morgan stepped out of her bath at about the same time that Captain Macready made up his mind to go ashore. As she rubbed under her breasts she abstractedly felt their weight with a small pleasurable ripple. She smoothed the towel down over her belly, vigorously drying her thighs and legs. She slipped on a wrap and walked into her bedroom. Below she heard a key in the door-lock.

'Is that you, Tegwyn?' she called in her low mellifluous voice.

'Uh huh,' her daughter called in the fashionable transatlantic syllables.

'Come up, will you?'

Friday was Tegwyn's night off from The Feathers. She came into her mother's bedroom and flopped down on the bed.

'What is it, Mother?' she asked.

'I was just wondering if you were coming dancing tonight?' replied Justine, sitting at her dressing-table and brushing her hair. At the same time she scrutinised her daughter for telltale signs. Tegwyn yawned and shrugged, then lay back and stretched like a cat. Her mother's eyes narrowed. There was fire in the belly of that one, thought Justine, as she saw the half-smile curl upon her daughter's lips.

'I might. And then again I mightn't.'

'And that means you will and you've designs upon some unsuspecting fellow.'

'Mother, how could you?' said Tegwyn, sitting up in mock indignation.

Justine stopped brushing her hair and stood up. Undoing her wrap she stepped into a pair of knickers. Tegwyn watched her mother's figure in admiration. An odd pang of unaccountable jealousy pricked her.

'And what if I am? You're not beyond a flirt yourself.'

Her mother threw off the wrap and began putting on her brassiere, deftly arranging her cleavage. She laughed.

'I'm old enough and wise enough not to get into trouble, my girl. I've seen you and that new Harbour Master making eyes at one another. He's unscrupulous, you know. A girl like you is not in his class but he'll use you and then when he's finished

101

he'll chuck you to one side.' She picked up a slip and a pair of stockings.

'Rubbish, Mother. I can take care of myself.'

'Just make sure you can, that's all. Now go and get ready. It's black tonight. I've a pair of black stockings you can borrow in the second drawer.'

Tegwyn got up from the bed. 'I've my own black stockings, thank you.' She flounced out of the room.

By the time he had been home and chatted to his wife over a cup of tea Captain Macready was late at the Tudor Tea Rooms where the dancing club held its weekly meeting. He was also unprepared for the sight that met his eyes.

In coupled pairs the members were dancing a tango under the direction of Justine Morgan as leading *danseuse*. Except that they were not exactly doing that. Only one couple was actually dancing while the others watched, and Justine, leaning on the gramophone with her lips slightly parted and a rapt expression on her face, took no part in directing the couple. For a minute the Captain gazed at Justine. He had never seen her so provocative off the floor. One hip jutted out, eloquently supported by one of those fine, sturdy legs. The other leg was in repose, her high-heeled shoe tap-tapping to the rhythm. Although still, her whole body seemed coiled round the music and it was only when the Captain realised she was motivated not so much by the beat of the tango as by the spectacle before her that he looked at the couple that was generating all the electricity.

Now at this precise point Septimus Macready had no idea who the young man was. He simply saw a broad-shouldered, fair-haired male, following the erotically formal movements of the tango to perfection. He was leading a splendidly arrogant girl whose out-thrust breasts seemed, in a nautical simile, like the bow wave to the curve of her throat. Her head was thrown back and a cascade of hair tumbled from a black ribbon done up on the crown of her head. For a second Macready was confused. The girl seemed a suddenly metamorphosed Justine, dancing with the mature confidence he so much admired. Then he realised it was Tegwyn and he too stood transfixed until the final chord and the abrupt halt to the dance.

A storm of quite spontaneous applause burst from the eight or nine couples standing about the tea room. Stanier and Tegwyn walked off the floor hand in hand like lovers from a formal dance floor. The others gathered round with cries of enthusiastic comment. Macready entered the room and went up to Justine.

'Sorry I'm late, m'dear. Damn ship's kept outside ...' he smiled, puzzled at the tears in her eyes. He had never seen tears such as these before. Tears of laughter quite a few times, but never of pathos. He blundered on, embarrassed at the effect they were having on him.

'I see we'll have to watch our laurels ... who is the young fellow?'

Justine had recovered herself and smiled. 'Him? Why I thought you'd know him.' She saw Macready frown slightly.

104

'He's the new Harbour Master, Captain Stanier, old Tom Edwardes' successor.'

'Well, I'll be damned. So he's the young jackanapes who got me locked out, is he?' It was Justine's turn to be surprised at her partner's expression.

'Septimus, what is it? You've gone quite red!'

He let out his breath in a long, slow exhalation. He shook his head. 'Nothing.'

Justine's eyes sparkled again. She touched Macready's arm. 'They danced well, though, didn't you think? Tegwyn was beautiful,' she finished in a whisper and Macready caught her mood, unconsciously setting words to his thoughts.

'Yes,' he said, his voice low and unusually sensual, 'she reminded me of you.'

Their eyes met and they exchanged a glance such as lovers of long standing exchange. And yet to them it was like the first time. For five years they had matter-of-factly danced with the team, a natural pair who danced together well. Between them there had never been the slightest hint of intimacy beyond the contacts prescribed by the formalities of various steps. Now something profound had occurred in that electric atmosphere of the Tudor Tea Rooms, in the shadow of aspidistras and piles of bentwood chairs.

Septimus Macready leant over and turned the handle of the gramophone. He lifted the needle and the record began to spin. He carefully lowered the needle and led Justine out to begin the tango. In the room the rest of the club turned from Stanier and Tegwyn, silence fell and the air crackled.

Aboard the *Caryatid* Bernard Foster finished his log book, completed his stores lists and sat back, relighting his pipe for the twentieth time. Along the alley-way Charlie still sat ruminating, lost in the fantasies of young, romantic love. It was uncanny the way he had preserved the feeling deep down inside himself that there was, in this tired old world, love such as the ancients enjoyed, such as poets wrote of and playwrights immortalised. Not for everyone, of course; the evidence of his experience suggested the vast majority of people rubbed along with a mixture of affection and lust. He mused on the problem, it probably explained the discontent apparently inherent in the human situation. He sighed with utter contentment. That he should be one of the lucky ones seemed incredible. And yet that tiny feeling of certainty he had experienced as he had looked west down the railway tracks had, despite himself and the cynical patina the years had laid upon him, been vindicated.

He spoke her name softly, whispering the syllables, laying emphasis upon differing parts of it, secretly teasing it with his tongue as he might her nipple.

The sun went down and about nine thirty a knock came on Charlie's cabin door. It was Mackerel Jack.

''Scuse me sir, we're ready to take the boat in for the lads.'

Charlie looked at his watch. 'Shore leave doesn't finish until eleven,' he said.

The seaman winked. 'I know sir. But we gen'rally run in a bit early, see, and wash our mouths out.' Charlie comprehended.

'Well, I'm not sure.'

'That's alright, Charlie,' it was Bernard's voice from the next cabin who was well aware of what was going on, 'we call it usage of the service—it's a long established tradition.'

Mackerel Jack smiled happily. Charlie smiled too. A few minutes later the launch left the ship's side. Charlie heard the hiss of spray as she plunged into a wave and thought that perhaps the wind had not moderated further.

In the Tudor Tea Rooms Macready had at last come face to face with Stanier. The Captain and Justine had danced the tango superlatively well. To the onlookers it had seemed a competitive performance; as if the older couple were confirming their right to remain the club's leaders, to re-establish their precedence in the pecking order.

As they finished, Stanier, who by now

knew the identity of the stocky well-built man dancing with Tegwyn's mother, walked over.

'My congratulations, Captain Macready. May I introduce myself? I'm James Stanier, the new Harbour Master.' He held out his hand, an urbane and charming smile upon his face.

Macready grunted. 'So you're the young jackanapes that locked my ship out tonight.' It was more a statement than a question.

'Sorry, Captain. Had a tidal job docking the *Sea Dragon;* you left it just too late getting your anchor up and ...' he shrugged, a peculiarly foreign gesture, or so Macready thought.

'Now you listen here, young man, don't you ever mess me or my crew about again. When I signal my ETA to the Coast Guard you make sure those damned gates are open. I'll worry about whether there's sufficient water on the sill, I'm a damned sight more familiar with this port than you are—' Justine watched, alarmed at the Captain's apoplectic colour. She turned and made violent 'come hither' motions to Miss Byford who looked after the tea arrangements. Miss Byford, who assisted Justine in her shop, was dressmaker to the club, a small, shrivelled, rather asexual little person with the energy of a ten-year-old boy. She bustled up and the intrusion of her tray with its cups and saucers and its ritual of 'Do you sugar, Captain Stanier? But of course Captain Macready doesn't,' at least soothed the irate Macready.

Stanier was unruffled by the outburst. That was the trouble with these Celts he thought, they never held their tempers long enough for their brains to work.

'I shall never give one ship preferential treatment, Captain, yours included. I should perhaps remind you, though this is scarcely the place for gentlemen to argue, that I *am* the Harbour Master of Porth Ardur.' Stanier sipped his tea.

Macready opened his mouth to speak, thought better of it and shut it again. He had not liked the inflection of the word 'gentlemen'.

'Perhaps, Captain Stanier, I could remind you, because I know Captain Macready is too much of a gentleman to do so himself, that as Master of the *Caryatid* he is a Harbour Commissioner for Porth Ardur.' Justine smiled warmly at the younger man. Macready's heart went out in gratitude to the lovely widow.

Stanier coloured and Tegwyn shot her mother a look of pure venom. However this sally had restored Macready's ruffled feathers and he tried, filled as he was with love, to pour oil on troubled waters.

'Come, come, Captain, if you'll be good enough to have the gates open in,' he looked at his watch, 'two and a half hours, we'll berth *Caryatid* and say no more about it.' He turned away and he and Justine lined up the club for one of their routines. It was only Tegwyn who heard Stanier mutter, 'I'm damned if I will.'

Those members of the *Caryatid*'s crew that had enjoyed a watch ashore usually assembled in the public bar of The Feathers about closing time for a quick half pint before they scrambled down to the boat. A few had spent the entire evening there and the boat's crew had been sinking pints for forty-five minutes.

Calico Jack had come ashore with the boat's crew and managed to consume eight swift glasses by the time the landlord called time. At ten twenty-nine Captain Macready had entered the lounge bar with Justine. They both had gin and tonics.

'You bringing her in tonight, Captain?' enquired the landlady serving them.

Macready nodded. 'I don't envy you that rowdy lot in the public.'

'They're alright. They do everything automatically.' The landlady sniffed. 'I'll go and cash up then.' She left them alone, for the rest of the bar was empty. The Captain looked at Justine and she smiled back.

'Thank you for putting that youngster down.' Her smile broadened. 'I didn't like the way he talked to you and I'm not sure I like what he's doing to Tegwyn.'

'I didn't know you really cared what

anybody said.' Oh dear, Macready thought, this sounds as hackneyed as a film. But he need not have worried.

Justine shrugged. 'I don't think I did until this evening.'

'Odd, isn't it? I mean, all these years we've known each other ...' he drew a deep breath, feeling like an adolescent, '... and I've never wanted to kiss you like I do now.' She looked up at him and he bent over her and very lightly, tentatively, half-expecting an outraged rebuff, he kissed her. Justine slowly opened her lips. Messages flashed from brain to brain, loins to loins, immediate urgent messages. But maturity triumphed and they drew apart before the landlady returned.

'Do you love your wife, Septimus?' asked Justine.

'Gwendolen?' he replied surprised. Justine laughed her open gay laugh that defused the question.

'Of course Gwendolen, you don't have any more, do you?' Justine laughed again. 'But do you love her?'

'We've been together a long time. It

becomes a sort of habit, I suppose. It's not a question that one often asks oneself ...'

'Or mentions?'

Macready shrugged, then nodded, I suppose not.'

It was Justine's turn to take a deep breath. 'Septimus, you are probably not going to believe this given my reputation, but since my husband died I have never slept with another man. Oh I've flirted, led them on, had them take me to dinner and the pictures but never ... you know ...' She was blushing now.

'I never believed those stories anyway ...' he began gallantly but she waved him to silence.

'Septimus, what I'm trying to say is will you ... do you want to sleep with me?' She buried her delicious mouth in her gin and tonic.

Macready had answered before he had thought about it—much as Stanier might have expected of an impetuous Celt: 'Yes!'

It was nearly time for the boat to leave and

the glasses were almost all emptied in the public bar.

Calico Jack was happily drunk and for the tenth time in the hour since he came ashore was telling the story about his island love being naked under an old fur coat. It would appear to have been the high spot of his life except that his ship-mates had heard other equally extravagant yarns. The landlord was thundering time and eventually *Caryatid*'s crew drifted out into the darkness towards the waiting boat.

They were singing lustily when Captain Macready descended the steps.

'It's alright, my dear,' said Stanier solicitously, 'I'll ask the clerk to get me a drink then, while he does so, up you go. He does it every night so he'll not think anything's amiss.'

Tegwyn looked up at the damp exterior of the Station Hotel. Damn her mother, she thought impetuously. She looked at Stanier. He was smiling at her, patiently, solicitously. A real gentleman.

She nodded. 'Alright.'

Deadly Sins

It was as well that at least one man in Porth Ardur that night committed the sin of disobedience. Thomas Jones, fully aware of the locking out of the *Caryatid*, braked his bicycle outside the Harbour Master's office at a quarter past twelve. He reappeared with a handful of oil lamps and disappeared into the rain-drenched darkness along the mole.

At least several of *Caryatid*'s crew therefore benefited by his action. It is true that had he not turned up, in accordance with Captain Stanier's instructions (to wit that no signals should be made to ships in the bay without his express order and presence on the quayside), what later occurred between Captain Macready and Justine might not have. But it is more likely that it would only have been postponed. In any event Jones's actions had no bearing on the frantic activity in the Station Hotel except to ensure that neither mother nor daughter discovered the other had slept out that night. So from that point of view Thomas Jones rendered a public service by retaining peace in one household. That he also indirectly sheltered Captain Stanier was not likely to be recognised by that overzealous young man as a personal service. But we anticipate.

Caryatid berthed at 0108 on the Saturday morning. Within minutes of securing her ropes she became like a morgue. The main engines were shut off and the fires banked. Even the steam generators were closed down and the 'bulkhead dynamos', as the oil lights were called, were lit by those remaining on board. Seamen and firemen, some in shore clothes, others in working dungarees, hurried ashore. Last to go was Bernard Foster. By the time he left, Charlie was stripping off and rolling into his bunk. For perhaps ten minutes *Caryatid* lay like a dead thing. Below, the nightwatchman poured himself another cup of tea, moved the oil lamp nearer the penny dreadful and idly wondered how long it would be before he dozed off.

At the end of those ten minutes a late observer might have noticed a movement in her wheelhouse and another in the shadows of the quay. But there were no observers, for the night was still blustery and another rain squall drove over the port. Even our first transgressor, Thomas Jones, had reached home and was at that moment letting his dripping self into his cottage.

Thus it was that Justine Morgan tripped across the gangway, aboard the *Caryatid* and into the waiting arms of Septimus Macready, unobserved by anyone save her eager lover. When they reached the cabin he took her coat. She threw off her scarf and shook her hair, kicking her shoes off in one sensuous movement. Her eyes were bright and he looked at her in admiration.

'Where did you wait? I'm sorry to have been so long!'

She giggled. 'You'll never guess.'

He shrugged. 'I've been waiting in the church,' she said. He laughed softly, 'Well

I'm damned ... ' then, realising what he had said, they both laughed softly together like conspiratorial children.

Justine could not truly say what made her enter the church for she was no practising Christian. But St Iseult's church stood just behind the buoy compound, slightly above the harbour and she knew it would be unlocked, for the vicar had views about the House of God remaining open. And in a way Justine needed that refuge, not just from the rain but for her soul. Great had been her love for her husband, so great that she had kept it as a memory so personal and intimate that only she and her husband's shade knew about it. And God, of course. There had to be God otherwise her husband's soul could not exist and her nocturnal practices would have been no more than self-abuse. She did not believe they were.

But something had happened tonight. She was not sure what, or that she wanted to know, except that the sight of her little daughter aroused and in the arms of a man had ignited some latent kindling in herself. The only man who occupied any sort of permanency in her life was Septimus Macready and seeing him there, she had suddenly realised that very sense of dependability that Septimus radiated was attractive. Of course, he had been attractive for years and it was this that their bodies had recognised from the start, this that had made them such superlative dancers, and fed the perceptive gossips of Porth Ardur.

For Septimus too, after half a century of life, he felt lust as painful and as sharp as his brief physical relationship with Gwendolen. His pores opened at the prospect before him. He turned the oil lights down very low and drew Justine into his tiny night cabin.

A deck below them Charlie Farthing slept. He dreamed of a holy land of heather that lay like velvet under his destrier's hooves. Stark granite outcrops pushed through the heather and there was a megalith older than measured time breaking the skyline. He felt his hauberk rasp his neck and his helmet, slung at his hip, rubbed his thigh, but the damp west wind was in his face and ahead of him lay the road to Avalon ...

Two decks down the nightwatchman slumped over the messroom table and dozed, dreaming of nothing ...

Justine lay back on the tiny bunk. Septimus leaned over her. He was trembling.

'My God, Justine, you are beautiful ...' She smiled at him, feeling her own flesh quivering. She felt the weight of her hips and parted her thighs as he knelt between them. He had a good body, she thought, still taut, a fine down of wiry hair across his square chest ... and lower down he was as eager as a boy.

Charlie Farthing dreamed on. His destrier was eager too, searching for the smell of a mare. The heather plateau went on and on. He searched himself, straining in the saddle for a sight of she whom he had come to seek. The destrier slid into a depression. As they rose on the farther side a standing stone came into view. They approached it and

121

suddenly the destrier whinnied. A pale horse stepped forward and upon it sat a green-eyed maiden, russet hair streaming in the wind. Charlie dismounted, clumsy in his harness, and knelt at her feet. The ground was hard, hard ... Charlie awoke on the deck, tangled in his bedclothes ...

At the Station Hotel Tegwyn was eagerly exhausting James Stanier. But the honour of a gentleman is sacrosanct in the discharge of his duties to a lady and Stanier was on her and off her in a welter of sexual abandon ...

At about the time that Charlie fell out of his bunk one other sinner was active. Calico Jack, being a practical man, had sinned deliberately and accepted the consequences of his action philosophically. Trained in the matter of sinning he was not so abandoned as to urinate in his bunk, but the consequences of his greed led him to rise from it. In any case his pillow had apparently been gently revolving around his head for upwards of an hour or so. He went to the head and emptied his bladder then crawled back along the alley-way only to see a half-empty bottle of whisky in the messroom. He staggered in and picked it up. He remembered some drollery about a pessimist seeing a bottle half-empty, while an optimist saw it half-full, and chuckled at his own optimism. Then he tipped it down his gullet.

The price of his greed was repaid with interest. The stream of his yellow vomit shot across the mess table and Calico Jack passed out on the deck.

Sins are usually reckoned to be actions that transgress arbitrary moral codes laid down by religious writ. Immoral acts, on the other hand, are less clearly defined since the viewpoint of the observer, or arbiter, has great bearing on the subject. It is generally accepted that an immoral act is one in which people are hurt, whether directly in the committing of the act, or indirectly as a consequence of the act.

Thomas Jones's action in disobeying Captain Stanier's order was a sin, since Stanier was his superior. But no church would condemn him for an act that he conceived a kindness to his friends on the *Caryatid*. Yet Stanier would be hurt by the act, his pride wounded, perhaps some bilious combination in his body's constitution would hasten his eventual demise by, perhaps, two minutes? Who knows?

But Stanier was young and would revenge himself if he was that upset, to pushing the treadwheel of human futility round another half-revolution.

The activity in the Station Hotel was another dance nearly as old as time, but it was a fornication, a sin the Celts indulged in themselves and condemned in others. But if no one was hurt where was the harm? If a child was the result of this union then condemnation might be justified, but Stanier was a young man with a high sense of his dignity. No one was going to trap him into a hasty marriage to legitimise a bastard and he, in his cold, Saxon loving, was too efficient to be totally overruled by lust.

But the sweet, ripe loving of Septimus and Justine carried with it the full knowledge that someone was most certainly going to be hurt if she found out. Gwendolen's shadow hung between them as a strange, dolorous barrier, giving to their love a piquant sadness, a foredoomed premonition that increased towards the morning.

At last Justine rose and cast about for her clothes. Macready watched her.

'Will we do this again, my dear?' he asked softly.

She shrugged, tears starting in her eyes, 'Oh yes, my darling, yes, yes ...' she sobbed in his arms. He stroked her hair as Justine pulled herself together. 'I've an idea,' she said, suddenly brightening in her old, cheerful way. 'Do you go anywhere where you could spend several nights?'

'You mean in the ship?'

'Mmmm.'

Macready thought. 'Ynyscraven, a little island about sixty miles away. But Justine, you couldn't come on board ...'

'No, no, silly. But I could take a holiday there and you could ... you know ...'

The idea caught his imagination and he

grinned delightedly, 'What a splendid—'

'But we'd have to be careful. I don't want a scandal in this place.' She pulled up her stockings and fastened them. Septimus caught a final view of her thigh as she pulled down her skirt.

'Alright,' he said. 'We'll carry on just as normal here. I'll try and work some sort of long job at the lighthouse on Ynyscraven.' She nodded, fastening her scarf. He held out her coat.

'I'll slip ashore alright,' she said. He saw her to the gangway. For a second the big oil lamp caught her face then she was gone in the night. Septimus returned to his cabin. On the deck a white patch caught his eye. Justine had left her panties. He caught them up, a smile upon his face. It was replaced by sudden worry. My God! What if Gwendolen found them, he thought, finding himself stuffing them in his pocket. Supposing that bloody gossip of a steward found them ...

He flung open his wardrobe. He was likely to wear any of his three uniforms ... ah! that was the answer. He pulled out his mess jacket and slipped the silky thing away.

Justine noticed the omission before she reached the end of the quay. A sudden panic seized her too. It was on just such details that marriages foundered, how could she have forgotten, she who was so careful about her appearance? But she had been as eager as a young virgin tonight, so perhaps there was some excuse. She shrugged, relying on Septimus's dependability and hurried up the steep street. She wondered if it were possible to conceive at their ages. She found herself smiling at the thought. She slipped into bed within twenty minutes of leaving the ship, and was fast asleep when Tegwyn let herself into the little stone cottage.

The Wages of Sin

Thomas Jones woke the following morning with that uneasy feeling that something was wrong. It was not a very disturbing feeling, more an itch marring the even tenor of his life. He stirred, the bedclothes twisting round him uncomfortably. He sat up irritably. And remembered.

Stanier.

God blast the Saxon boor, but Stanier would want to know why, contrary to his orders, the *Caryatid* lay in the harbour.

Jones swore again and rose to put on a kettle and brew a cup of tea. While thus occupied he had an idea. It was not an original idea, most recently it had been propounded by the founder of the Boy Scouts movement but was older than Jones's Celtic warrior forbears. Certainly Stanier's Saxon antecedents had outwitted those same forbears and with that recollection Jones resolved to act. He would attack. On impeccable military authority it was the finest form of defence. Thus Thomas Jones turned aside the wrath of Captain Stanier and was able to avoid any retribution for his disobedience.

In truth Jones's own action did not really avert Stanier's wrath. Tegwyn Morgan had already done that. James St John Stanier lay abed late, replete with loving and satiated with recollection. Jones' note (that there were no intended movements other than the berthing of the *Caryatid* to which he would be pleased to attend without bothering the Captain) hardly had any effect upon Stanier who had already resolved not to stir from his bed for several hours. He slipped into sleep smiling.

After years of moral behaviour Captain Macready found his conscience irksome throughout the weekend. His was not a nature that dissembled easily. He bumbled solicitously after his wife, like a gull in a ship's wake, but that worthy woman, practical to the end, simply assumed he was unwell. She therefore reciprocated by mollycoddling him which increased his guilt. It was with considerable relief that Macready found himself climbing the stairs to bed on Sunday evening in the knowledge that when he next woke he could escape to the clean sea air which forgave the sins of men as being things of little moment.

Neither was it part of his wife's make up to enquire closely into her spouse's motivation. If he accepted her ministrations then she assumed she must be alleviating the ailment. With that little touch of martyr's wormwood she knew that by Monday Septimus would, like Richard on the morning of Bosworth, be himself again.

It was left to Calico Jack to pay in full the wages of sin. His hangover on Saturday morning was prodigious. Not even a pint with a whisky chaser bought in the public bar of The Feathers at eleven o'clock sharp, cleared the pain from his head. Calico Jack was, however, inured to such pain. Years of dedicated drinking had made him accept the consequences with a degree of stoicism that would have done credit to Epictetus had that worthy not disapproved of the cause.

The *Caryatid* was the latest in an incredibly long list of ships that had provided Jack with home and employment for half a century. Alone among them *Caryatid* also promised him the golden hope of a pension, for Calico Jack was one of a breed of men who toiled in the boiler rooms of steamers for decades and, at the end of the day, when their sinews were weakened and their breath came in pants, could walk ashore with their entire possessions in the bottom of a half-filled kit-bag.

To such a man drinking had become as much a way of life as another's fortnightly visits to the public library or the golf course. Calico Jack had drunk in every corner of this tired old earth; could be relied upon for a verdict on the inebriative qualities of alcoholic beverages from arrack to ouzo, and could tell you where, in each sailortown from Archangel to Yokohama, you could purchase the *vin du pays*.

It was not the worst hangover that Jack had ever experienced but there were other, more disturbing symptoms that his 'liveners' in The Feathers soon masked. Calico Jack did not know that the malfunctioning of his liver was reaching a critical point. It could not be said that he drank to forget pain, only that when he drank somehow he just forgot anyway.

So he spent his weekend in customary fashion. Having no family in Porth Ardur he slept aboard the ship and spent most of his waking hours, not to mention his entire weekly wage, in The Feathers.

But it should not be thought that Calico Jack was a simple man for his fund of experience ran back too far and was too diverse for that. Even at his age he was not without a certain vivacity. He surprised many a youthful engineer by reciting lengthy sections of romantic poetry such as it had once been fashionable to cram into the heads of infants at Board Schools. Jack had received most of his education in the great Varsity of the World which is the unequivocal *alma mater* of every merchant seaman.

Neither was Jack an unhappy man. He was the most undeceived of all men, knowing full well that naked he had come into this world and naked he would go out of it. Perhaps that was the root of his philosophy, for he worked hard, in the primeval conditions of a stokehold, his lean body corroded without by coal dust and sweat, and within from a great universality of booze. And he played hard, as much a part of the great rut as the Canadian moose, and far more honestly than James Stanier. Certainly Calico Jack had loved. He had been the victor of many an affray with bar and brothel girl; he boasted of having done the impossible with the unspeakable (or was it the other way round?) and had collected several scars to prove it. But best of all he nurtured the memory of his first voyage when, as a boy of fourteen, he had shipped out on a whaler that had called unexpectedly at the fishing port where he lived. Jack had sailed in her

133

on a four-year cruise into the wide blue Pacific and there he had been privileged to love a dusky maiden. He was one of the last of those old sailormen who had stormed their way into that promiscuously innocent ocean and despoiled its islands with a truly Viking ferocity, taking spirits and syphilis into the lives of the innocently, charmingly compliant natives. In the cruise the whaler had five times recruited in the Marquesas and Calico Jack, the least significant figure on that old auxiliary barque, had disported himself with the carnality that adolescence and too much bad adult example produced.

But Jack had not simply lusted in the Marquesas. He had loved, absolutely, romantically, even fantastically. For he had discovered his maiden bathing in a pool, had seduced her, or been seduced by her, and they had lived and loved under those tropic skies of dark velvet for three delirious weeks. And thus it had been on each visit, until the whaler turned for home, her holds crammed with the sperm oil that industry then wanted. Jack had felt sorrow at his last departure, half-promising to return, half-knowing he would not. He had seen during those five visits the waist of his woman thicken, had seen small dusky children multiply about the island, and seen her breasts lose their pointed sauciness so that his passion had cooled. In that early initiation into the natural law of decay lay his determination to wander; yet the memory of that first, pure love came to him now as an old and almost broken man. It shone in his memory as Rigel Kentaurus had burned in that Marquesan firmament all those years ago.

It was this stirring of this memory that caused him to think himself in love with the madwoman of Ynyscraven. *Caryatid*'s crew had known Sonia's mother for years as the 'madwoman'. The old lady had lived on the island for about fifteen years, arriving one day on a fishing boat with three cabin trunks and a small child. She was some kind of artist and considered a harmless lunatic. The islanders all liked her daughter and she was inoffensive, paid her debts and kept out of anyone's way.

For a long time she had always exchanged greetings with Calico Jack, even danced with him once or twice. They seemed to be capable of sitting silently together, wrapped in each other's company, though exchanging not a word. It was clear to even the most mule-headed observer that they were both slightly cracked. Or perhaps they knew they had both drunk at a well of loneliness and suffering that those who have visited, never afterwards mention.

It was love that triumphed over Calico Jack's physical decay that weekend, and Sunday night found him again staggering from The Feathers in time to flash up the two scotch boilers and raise steam for Monday's tide.

It is a curious quality of divine retribution that it is often absent from those whom others think best deserve it. In the neat stone cottage that housed Mrs and Miss Morgan there was no hint of sin or its concomitant consequences. Indeed both women were able to maintain that ambiguous attitude to their individual behaviour that chiefly characterises their sex from that of the simpler, more brutal male.

Both women considered they were in love. This in the first place exonerated all subsequent peccadilloes. In Justine's case it was probably true, whereas in Tegwyn's, love was not quite the right word. Nevertheless from the individual standpoint their hearts sang in their ample breasts that no woman had ever loved like this before.

But there lurked the tiny worm of guilt, a particularly Celtic worm, for it fed on other people's good opinion, and therefore the Morgan household was one of extraordinary amity and concord as daughter sought to please mother and mother tried to make up for that gap in her maternal vigilance that had occurred as she lay in the hairily masculine arms of Septimus Macready. As a consequence of their individual preoccupations with these deceptions, neither noticed anything odd about the other's behaviour and the weekend passed very pleasantly. This alone they attributed to being in love, each thinking only she was experiencing it, which circumstance fed their own self-conceit delightfully.

Men who rarely mar the even tenor of their lives, rarely experience the pangs and expectations of adventurous souls. This was true of Bernard Foster, whose weekend consisted of a dutifully performed sexual coupling with his wife, a walk with two sons and a spaniel and a duty visit to the ship to pick up Charlie Farthing for 'a quiet Sunday evening with my family'.

It is not true to say that Bernard lacked a sense of humour. His spaniel, for instance, was called Windlass. One, because it was a bitch, and two, because of an unfortunate propensity it had for breaking wind in public. His wife did not quite see the joke, however, which was becoming increasingly true of poor Anthea's whole outlook on life. But Bernard was a dedicated father, a good seaman who enjoyed his work and a pipe smoker. None of these occupations, particularly the last which consumed vast quantities of matches, seemed to leave much time for excessive hilarity.

Charlie's visit was a success. He was good company and presentable enough to cause Anthea to take some pains with her appearance, so that Bernard felt a trifle jealous of young Charlie ... Oh well, he sighed and reached for his matches.

Alliances Are Made

The next few weeks passed with only a few catspaws disturbing the tranquillity of Porth Ardur. Since few of these were in any way public, no one could have supposed that there was anything amiss in the town.

There had been an unpleasant interview aboard *Caryatid* between Captain Stanier and Captain Macready. For once the former's cool headedness had deserted him as he had chosen to bait Macready on the latter's home ground. Voices were raised and it was difficult for both Foster and Charlie not to hear what was being said. Charlie Farthing listened with particular interest since his name, not to mention his manners, seemed to be the chief topic of Stanier's complaint. It is true that by the time Stanier had finished, Charlie's appearance and demeanour had been unfavourably linked with Macready's, and *Caryatid* had been reduced in maritime importance to less than a Thames lighter, but in so doing Stanier signed his own death warrant. Charlie could not understand why Foster kept digging him in the ribs as the two officers stood like schoolboys at the foot of the companionway leading up to the bridge. Suddenly he realised Stanier was pushing Macready onto ground which the older man regarded as highly contestable. At last Macready began to reply as Stanier ran out of steam. Charlie listened spellbound and next to him Bernard Foster was fairly hopping up and down with a glee that Charlie had not suspected of him.

'... And in future, Macready, I'll trouble you to take note of the fact that I'm in charge here, that you and this old coal-bucket you call a ship berth here by courtesy of the fact that the port allows it and don't think you can frighten me by waving your commissioner's badge at me because you only sit on the board by courtesy of the Parliamentary Act as a *representative* of the Lighthouse Authority and that cuts no ice with me. I remain the Harbour Master and you'd better not forget it!'

There was a pause, then:

'Mr,' (Macready emphasised that title derogating it as only a Celt can when mouthing the English tongue), 'Mr Stanier, I have stood here and listened to your bloody nonsense long enough. In my opinion, which is based on the trifle of thirty-nine years on this coast, Mr Farthing is as promising a young officer as *I* could wish for. If he failed to come up to your passenger-liner expectations I suggest you return to poodle-faking on promenade decks and fornicating with the cargo rather than running down *my* officers on *my* ship after you have exercised your trifling authority by locking this vessel out quite unnecessarily. You quite plainly demonstrate your complete inability to command anything larger than a motor launch by your pettiness and if I hear another word from you, sir, I shall have you forcibly removed from this vessel.

D'you understand me, damn it, for I'm going out on this tide and be damned to you!'

Neither Charlie nor Foster heard Stanier utter another word but they both stood smirking in the alleyway as the apoplectic features of James St John Stanier passed them.

For some time after this the *Caryatid* entered and left Porth Ardur as she had done for years. Macready assumed that Stanier had grown up and even went so far, by way of conciliation, as to smile at the brick caboose. Stanier, however, saw this as a gesture of defiance and pondered on the possibility of revenge.

To this end he was unexpectedly assisted from an unusual source and fell to more pondering as to how to put new allies to the best use. In part this deepening of the feud between the two men was caused by Gwendolen Macready. It was an inadvertent move on her part but was nevertheless instrumental in driving an influential party into Stanier's camp.

For many years the housewives of Porth

Ardur had complained about the excessive amount of sooty black smoke that spewed from *Caryatid*'s funnel as she fired up and steamed out of Porth Ardur on a Monday morning. This unfortunate emission often coincided with the hanging out of a vast acreage of sheets and pillow slips, not to mention unmentionables. Several times deputations had besieged the Lighthouse Authority office where the head clerk, untrained in the best methods of putting down riots by irate women, had locked himself in his office until the fuming crowd had dispersed. Protests to Captain Macready himself had been made, but the Captain had simply deplored the occurrence and mentioned it to the Chief Engineer. That worthy was a bachelor and did not give a monkey's damn about all the women in the world, since one had once infected him with the clap. He therefore did nothing about it except smile savagely and recollect that Calico Jack was usually on duty when *Caryatid* sailed since he lived aboard. This fact would happily ensure that the practice continued to torment the goodwives of Porth Ardur.

The wives, many of whom were married to men in *Caryatid*'s crew, had tried various ploys including one inspired by Lysistrata and her friends. This had, however, been a one-sided sacrifice that had led to several nasty bedroom mêlées, not to mention a revealing argument in the queue of Beynon's Butchery. Consequently it had been abandoned. The simple expedient of washing on a Tuesday never seemed to occur to any of the parties concerned, unless it was a matter of principle, in which case neither party could, in all honour, compromise.

Something of Macready's disagreement with Stanier reached the ears of Gwendolen through the agency of Anthea Foster. Gwendolen attributed her husband's preoccupation to this cause and not to any burgeoning romance with Justine. Mrs Macready in turn made enquiries about Captain Stanier in her own circles. It seemed common knowledge that the new broom was sweeping clean and she let slip an innocent remark that her husband seemed to be receiving something of the treatment. This was quickly seized upon by Mrs Beynon, the butcher's wife, who astutely saw in it an opening ripe for exploitation by the careworn wives of Porth Ardur.

In the days of Captain Edwardes they had no luck in attempts to get the Harbour Master on their side. Captain Stanier, on the other hand, seemed to be a different proposition and Mrs Beynon quickly whipped up some support. The ladies deputed to approach the Captain swallowed their dislike of him being an 'outsider' and reflected that he was a handsome embellishment to the social scene and might be worthy of their daughters. A deputation therefore met the Captain at the Station Hotel where he generously bought them all gin and tonics.

'Now ladies, what exactly is it that I can do for you?' he began, his masculinity asserting control at the outset. He smiled urbanely round at the circle of faces.

'It's like this, see, that old ship makes a

great deal of smoke and we ladies, all of us, that is ...' The problem was outlined to Captain Stanier who, though privately nursing a snigger, agreed the ladies had a point of view and promised most sincerely to consider what he could do to help them.

It proved a difficult problem for the young man. To be fair he had little time for such considerations since his affair with Tegwyn was still burning with an incandescent fire. Besides he had another problem, that of accommodation.

Under the terms of his employment he was allowed a month in an hotel after which he was expected to make his own arrangements. He eventually settled on a furnished house in the poshest part of Porth Ardur: Glendŵr Avenue. This tree-lined road with its neat rows of Victorian villas was ideal for Stanier's self-esteem, compensating him in part for his miserable brick caboose. The house's owners were on extended service in the colonies and the place was full of oriental bric-a-brac which exactly fostered Stanier's image of himself as a great white empire builder. It was also a delightful place for further fornication with the beautiful Tegwyn who adorned a tigerskin rug so delightfully. Stanier had never realised that a stool made from an elephant's foot could be such an object of sexual stimulus or that an oxhide shield and an assegai could be used for erotic purposes.

All in all, despite the unpleasantness with Macready, Stanier was beginning to feel established in Porth Ardur.

This sensation was augmented by the presence of Sir Hector Blackadder who had arrived in the middle of June to inspect his refitted yacht. *Sea Dragon* was a modern diesel yacht 105 feet long. Sir Hector was very proud of her and usually manned her from the unemployed of Porth Ardur who, desperate for work, were capable of debasing themselves with sufficient submission to please the millionaire and make him justify the maintenance of *Sea Dragon* as a kind of employment institution for the deprived.

Not that Sir Hector should be considered

a hard man. He lived in times when such simple ideas were quite permissible, indeed a large section of the town's population agreed with him and regarded him as a benefactor. This further pleased Sir Hector who regarded capitalists as the new aristocracy and was rather fond of saying this in public. He was equally fond of saying that anyone could get where he was if he worked hard, and that his knighthood had been conferred by an impressed monarch as encouragement to others of his class. He was never heard to explain how he had started to amass his fortune but there had been a story current in Porth Ardur when Sir Hector first started holidaying there, that he had always gone to school with a pair of scissors. With these he had snipped flowers from middle-class gardens and after school had stood innocently outside hospital gates reproaching empty-handed expectant fathers with masses of chrysanthemums and irises.

Whatever the origins of his wealth it was now legendary and Sir Hector regarded it as incumbent upon himself to own a yacht. Although the proprietor of the Cambrian Steam Navigation Company owned twenty-three rusting and profitable ships he was not overfamiliar with matters nautical. He therefore found it necessary to employ a yacht-master and it was with this in mind, as well as to inspect his recently refitted yacht, that he had come to Porth Ardur.

While he was walking round the yacht Stanier had strolled along the quay and, of course, introduced himself.

'Are you a master mariner, Captain?'

'But of course, Sir Hector.'

'What company were you with?'

'Isthmus and Occidental, sir,' replied Stanier, slightly outraged that the other should have to ask the question. After all there was the I&O and there was the rest of the Merchant Marine ...

'Ever consider serving in the Cambrian Steam Navigation Company?'

Stanier sensed a trap and looked quickly at Blackadder. The millionaire was regarding him with a level, inquisitive gaze.

'No, sir.'

'I suppose you've heard it has a few old and rusty ships that feed badly and hire and fire indiscriminately ... come now is that it?'

Stanier smiled deprecatingly and shrugged, 'Something like that, Sir Hector ...' Blackadder laughed, 'Well at least you are honest. It may be true, Captain, but they are profitable ships. I *know* they make more profit per voyage than your I&0 liners and, in the long term, that's what matters. If the I&0 lost its government mail contracts it would fold in ten years. Yes, it would. Don't protest.'

'Well, that's unlikely Sir Hector.'

'Don't be a damned fool, it'll end in two years once the aeroplane takes over, that's the field to watch next. I'm considering expanding into it myself.' Sir Hector raised his gaze above the rooftops of Porth Ardur and the mountains beyond as if searching for an aeroplane amid the cumulus. It was the look of a visionary.

He returned his gaze to Stanier. 'Would you like a job here, Captain?'

'I'm sorry, Sir Hector, I don't understand?'

'Oh I know you're tied up here but you must be due some summer leave. I'm inviting you to take a working holiday as master of the *Sea Dragon*. You can plan a three week cruise around the coast here, there are some lovely spots. What d'you say?'

'Well, Sir Hector, I'd like it very much but ...'

'But me no buts, Captain, I've a little influence hereabouts that can get you time off. You can dine at my table and bring your wife, d'you have a wife, Captain?'

'Er, no, Sir Hector.'

'I don't doubt an I&0 officer like you has fixed himself up in Porth Ardur, eh?'

Stanier grinned, 'Well as a matter of fact I, er—'

'That's settled then, as long as she doesn't eat peas off a knife and knows the difference between champagne and claret she'll be alright. Is she pretty?' Stanier coloured, thinking of Tegwyn and the assegai. 'Oh alright, Captain, I'm sure she is, just fix her up with a decent evening dress and bring her along, Now, let's have dinner at my hotel this evening and we can discuss details, bring a chart up with you ...' And so Captain James St John Stanier was officially appointed to his first sea-going command.

By the time June turned to July several sets of plans had been made in Porth Ardur. Stanier, Blackadder and Tegwyn Morgan were preparing to sail during the first week in August. Stanier had not found it easy to persuade Tegwyn, for she would openly acknowledge her liaison with Stanier by sailing on the *Sea Dragon*. Tegwyn knew many of the crew of the yacht would raise eyebrows at her presence, so she hit upon the idea of going as Stanier's guest and made much noise about the formality of the invitation. She was still apprehensive about telling her mother but was amazed by the reaction when she eventually did so.

'Of course, *cariad,* you go and enjoy yourself I shall shut up the shop, I think, and take a few days off myself.' Justine smiled at her daughter. 'You'll need some evening clothes in the latest mode ... we'll see what we can do there.'

'Oh Mother, you are absolutely wonderful!' Tegwyn threw her arms around Justine.

But Justine's heart leapt on her own account. When she next saw Septimus at the Friday dance she gave him the go-ahead for their own plot. As they left the Tudor Tea Rooms she hurriedly whispered the dates she hoped to be on Ynyscraven.

'How will you get there, my dear?' asked Macready.

'I'll take a train to Aberogg; that's where the mail boat goes from, isn't it?'

Macready nodded, smiled and squeezed her arm.

'It's not long to wait now, my dear.'

'No, my darling, not long.'

Charlie Farthing had seen Sonia several times since that first meeting and was more in love with her than ever. The *Caryatid* had spent odd afternoons working at the lighthouse on Ynyscraven and Sonia had appeared over the crest of the island every time he had landed. They had exchanged kisses and meaningless endearments while the *Caryatid*'s seamen exchanged leers, winks and suggestive gestures.

Charlie was delighted when Captain Macready mentioned they would be spending some time at the island in August.

'We'll be renewing the hoist wire at Ynyscraven in August. It'll mean at least a week there. That should please you, Mr Farthing.' Macready smiled, nursing the greater part of the smile for himself.

'Yes, sir, it does indeed.'

After the Captain had gone below, Charlie asked Foster what exactly was involved. Foster lit his pipe and puffed.

'Well, we have to cut the old wire out and remove it, then stretch a new one, cut and splice it, set it up taut. When that's done we renew the traveller and hoisting wire itself. It's a big job. If everything goes alright, five days. If we get any snags it may take longer.' He puffed again. 'When that's all set up, the engineers will overhaul the hoisting engine. They can't do that while we are working since we need it to heave things about. They'll start when we've finished. That'll take two days, so we'll probably be the weekend away. All the wives'll moan but the lads'll have a great time. The Old Man won't work after six o'clock, so by seven the boat'll be away to the pub,' he puffed again, 'and you'll be in seventh heaven.' Foster smiled at Charlie who grinned back.

'Sounds like a bloody holiday,' he said ingenuously.

'It's bloody hard work; you earn any free time you get.'

In this way plans were laid by the various parties for their own pleasure and amusement. Anticipation ran high in the breasts of those involved. Several members of *Caryatid*'s crew were delighted with the news, Calico Jack chief among them. Justine Morgan congratulated herself on the way things had turned out while Tegwyn, writhing in the uncontrollable excesses of sexual abandon, furnished herself with a wardrobe not strictly for evening wear from the more outrageous recesses of her mother's shop.

Stanier approached the whole exercise as a cold professional. He acted as though it were the *Mauretania* that he was taking command of and subconsciously relegated Tegwyn to the status of a passenger. It has to be remembered that James St John Stanier had had a surfeit of passengers.

Macready happily prepared for several nights of idyllic love and salved his conscience by busying himself around the, house during the intervening weekends, tidying up a number of jobs that Gwendolen had long ago abandoned any hope of getting him to do.

And Charlie Farthing dreamed dreams of love ...

This euphoric state of affairs might have continued until the *Caryatid* and the *Sea Dragon* sailed from Porth Ardur and the Ynyscraven mail boat slipped out of Aberogg, had not an unforeseen event occurred which upset the judgement of one of the vessels' commanders and ruined the equanimity of another.

A Declaration of War

Clausewitz maintained that war was the continuation of diplomacy by other means. If by diplomacy he meant the posturing of factions whose ambitions are in opposition, then he may have been right. War is war whether at the international level or around the parish pump and it follows the usual pattern of human disagreement, a series of small incidents that culminate in an outbreak of hostilities. But historians like a *casus belli* and it should not be supposed that this factor was absent from the clash of personalities that ruptured the peace of Porth Ardur.

A few days prior to commencing his cruise with Sir Hector, Stanier had decided to take the field against Macready. His alliances were holding and a curious piece of information had come his way. Armed with this intelligence, which he considered to be an irresistible reinforcement, he intended to attack Macready over the distressing matter of *Caryatid*'s boiler smoke. Stanier smiled to himself as he walked down from Glendŵr Avenue that morning. He could see the harbour below him and *Caryatid*'s tall woodbine funnel belched black smoke which the wind caught and drove inland, up the shallow valley where the majority of the population lived.

His smile turned to a grimace as ahead of him he caught a glimpse of the stocky rolling figure of Captain Macready dressed in reefer jacket, with its bars of braid, and a small crowned hat, its peak adorned with the 'scrambled egg' that denoted a vessel's commander.

'Bloody charlatan,' muttered Stanier, recollecting the conversation he had had with Sir Hector Blackadder.

He had dined quite frequently with Sir Hector when the millionaire had come down for a weekend to Porth Ardur. The talk had been of the forthcoming cruise and Sir Hector had been enlarging on the manning of his yacht.

'Oh, the crew are never a problem,' said Sir Hector, puffing on a large Havana. 'You see, I bring the cook and cabin staff, they're my own permanent domestics. The engineer I retain, as you know, almost full-time. The couple of greasers and six seamen I pick up every year from the unemployed fishing hands hereabouts. The problem comes when I want a skipper ... '

Stanier winced at the terminology but Sir Hector ploughed on through a haze of blue smoke, unaware at the savage knocking the younger man's pride had just received.

'Usually I get someone in the port who's on leave, between ships and run out of money, old Edwardes often knew of someone with a ticket of some description. Of course they don't all get invited to dine at my table,' he smiled at Stanier who smiled back, his wounded pride salved a little.

'And none of the previous skippers have *ever* been invited to bring their mistress.' Sir Hector drew on the Havana.

'I'm very flattered, Sir Hector ... '

Sir Hector grunted. Then he looked up. 'I like you, Stanier, you've a ruthless streak and I'm on the lookout for a junior partner.'

'I'm, er, quite overwhelmed Sir Hector, I, er ...'

The knight bachelor waved aside the younger man's protestations of undying loyalty. 'We'll see, we'll see ... anyway as I was saying, it has often been a problem since I don't really know a great deal about navigation and I'm advised the tides hereabouts are rather tricky. One year I had a dreadful chap. Name of Evans, not that that means much round here. He was the best old Edwardes could trawl up for me. He was a damned trawler skipper. Swore he was the finest skipper on the coast but'd had a disagreement with his owner. Trouble was I'd not much time to check his credentials and I had a rather lovely Italian contessa in the party and my judgement was, huh,' Sir Hector laughed condescendingly as if about to reveal a great secret, 'well, impaired. Don't ever let a woman impair y'r professional judgement, young fella. It don't do and the bloody damage is done before you realise it.' Sir Hector puffed again at the cigar.

'The stupid bastard got us tangled in among some rocks with a tide race running like a river in spate. Beautiful afternoon somewhere down off that lighthouse, the, er, whatsitsname? Bucka-something ...'

'Buccabu, Sir Hector. Decanter?'

'Buccabu! That's it! Er yes lad, not a bad port, eh, even for this place. Buccabu. I shall never forget it. I thought we'd had it. I smelt a rat when the bloody fool was in the wheelhouse with a bottle of rum but, Christ alive, we were in the middle of hell then. White water all around us hissing and sucking at us. The *Sea Dragon* generates nine hundred and eighty-six horse-power and it was like farting against thunder ...'

Sir Hector drew courage from his port glass, blenching at the recollection.

'What happened?' asked Stanier, fascinated. All this was so far from the ordered bridge routine of an I&O liner.

'One of the seamen burst into the wheelhouse, said he knew the place and would pilot us through and would one of us throw the bloody skipper off the bridge and take the wheel. Well, I couldn't steer but I had no compunction about getting that old soak off the bridge. When I turned round there was my beautiful contessa, her hair flying and her arms spinning that teak wheel as the sailor shouted directions from the bow. I can see her now,' Sir Hector gazed at the whorls and arabesques hanging almost motionless above the table as the cigar smoke rose languidly.

'God, but she was stunning. Her eyes cracked fire and she had nostrils that dilated when she was excited,' he sighed nostalgically. 'Turned out she'd been an Olympic yachtswoman. Ever since then I've taken a trick at the wheel.' He drew on the cigar butt then ground it out.

'I hope that you are not expecting any such excitement on this cruise, Sir Hector,' said Stanier also stubbing out his cigar.

'Not of that nature,' said Sir Hector winking lasciviously.

'But I should have thought one of the *Caryatid*'s mates might have been a suitable candidate,' volunteered Stanier, pouring another glass of port.

Blackadder shook his head. 'They get little leave although Foster brought *Sea Dragon* round here. That's when he found out about their lighthouse service. By the way, d'you know old Macready?'

Stanier made a face. 'Yeees,' he said warily.

Sir Hector smiled. 'Funny man. Been in those ships man and boy, I believe. He always looks more of the typical skipper than any of the lot I employ, what do you think?'

Stanier was flushed with the wine. 'He's all wind and a brass-bound uniform. Struts about that old coal bucket like an admiral. I don't suppose he's been anywhere other than round this coast.'

'You're right there, my boy. Old Macready hasn't a Board of Trade ticket to his name. Are you surprised? It's true! He comes from a generation that didn't need 'em, but don't be fooled. He knows his onions where seamanship's concerned.'

James St John Stanier missed the

last remark. His inebriated heart was singing in his breast, for now he had a weapon with which to chastise the upstart, charlatan Captain Septimus Bloody Ebb-Tide Macready.

The recollection of that conversation put vigour into Captain Stanier's stride as he fairly flew over the cobbled approach to the harbour. His lip curled derisively as he passed alongside the white-washed granite wall of the Lighthouse Authority's compound.

Thomas Jones met him with the morning's sailings. 'Usual stuff Cap'n; fishing boats and the *Carry* at high water. Macready's sent along to say that he'll leave the moment there's water on the sill, some emergency buoy job on the Hellweather ...'

'Yes, yes, very good, Mr Jones. Now I'm going aboard the *Caryatid*. I've a thing or two to say to Captain Macready.' He turned on his heel and strode off towards the gangway of the *Caryatid*. Behind him Jones chuckled.

Captain Macready was also in fine spirits. In the first place he was deliriously happy with anticipation. The approaching sojourn of *Caryatid* at Ynyscraven and the prospect of five whole nights with Justine almost caused him physical pain. Secondly it was a beautiful morning and the Captain had come to appreciate such things lately. Finally the challenge of an emergency job always stimulated him. It was with an impish delight therefore that the Captain riffled the papers on his desk and stared down onto the foredeck where the hands were securing a new buoy for the Hellweather Bank. He hummed light-heartedly, a man utterly contented with the world.

Captain Macready was vaguely aware of some cloud looming on the horizon of his dreams as the noise of a disturbance penetrated his conscious mind. Somewhere below an argument had begun. The Captain listened. He recognised Foster's voice, low and reasonable.

'But I am sorry, Captain, we are sailing as soon as possible and Captain Macready is rather busy. Captain, I really must insist ... '

'Get out of my way, man, who the devil d'you think you are?'

There was a scuffling noise then a pounding of feet on the companionway and Captain Stanier pulled back the door curtain from Macready's cabin.

Macready was still standing at the porthole. He turned slowly and confronted the invader. Stanier was hot from his argument with Foster and catching his breath from a too-quick ascent of the ladder.

'Ah, Captain Stanier, good morning. I am sorry they did not teach you to knock at cabin doors when you were an apprentice ...' Macready watched with pleasure as Stanier's flush deepened. But the man quickly recovered both his breath and his composure.

'My apologies, Captain Macready, but I wished to speak to you before you sailed and your chief mate has been less than helpful.'

Macready shrugged. 'Well, what can I do for you?'

'Would you mind stepping out onto your boat deck for a moment, Captain?'

There was a persuasive plausibility about Stanier that disarmed Macready. The Captain was not to know that the Harbour Master had planned his approach as he had walked down to the harbour.

The two men emerged onto the boat deck. Stanier looked up. *Caryatid*'s tall buff funnel rose above them, flanked by two enormous cowl ventilators. From the brass whistle the permanently leaking steam escaped with a faint hiss. The steam was white, the condensing vapour the colour of samite, pure against the pall of dense black smoke that spewed out in thick convolutions of partially-consumed carbon. It rose, then spread out, drifting sulkily away over the rooftops of Porth Ardur.

'*That*, Captain Macready, is what I wished to see you about.' Stanier's gesture was dramatic. It was the first piece of histrionic display he had allowed himself since he arrived.

'*That* is what I have received constant complaints about since taking my post as Harbour Master. I have to insist that you instruct your engineers and firemen that making that much smoke is entirely unnecessary ... it is quite obvious that the rudiments of stoking are unknown to your staff.'

Macready was willing to tolerate the complaint about the smoke, even from Stanier. He accepted the criticism since it was not new and had clearly been resurrected by persons who considered the new Harbour Master was able to help them. He was even prepared to meet Stanier half way and say that he would investigate the matter. But he was not prepared to accept *any* criticism of *Caryatid* or her ship's company. There was only one person qualified to carry out such a task and that was the person of her master, Captain Septimus Macready himself.

'Why, you young jackanapes, what in God's name gives you the idea that you could stoke a boiler one whit better than that?' Macready delivered the last word with such vehemence that a blob of spittle hit Stanier.

Macready waited for the younger man's reply, his face colouring rapidly as he prepared further invective. But Stanier was a model of Saxon coolness.

'Captain,' he replied, labouring the title with heavy sarcasm, 'I hold a Master's certificate. You do not. I scarcely think *you* are in a position to lecture me on anything!' he stared at Macready triumphantly.

Macready let out his breath slowly. He was discomfited. Beaten. The wind he had saved to blast this whippersnapper from the holy ground of *Caryatid*'s deck exhaled itself so that he seemed to shrink. With a great effort he struggled to draw another breath. Between clenched teeth he hissed at Stanier, 'Get off my ship ...' and trusting himself no longer he blundered back into the accommodation.

Stanier strutted slowly from the *Caryatid*. It was indeed a perfect morning.

Macready slumped on his settee. Stanier's barb had struck his heart. Not even the thought of Justine's body could lift this sudden depression. This was how Foster found him when he came to report the ship ready for sailing.

'Are you quite alright, sir?' he enquired anxiously, bending over the inert, crushed figure.

'Eh? Oh, er, yes, yes of course I am.'

'Shall I ring the engines to "Stand-by"?'

'What? Oh, yes, by all means; go ahead.'

With a great effort Macready pulled himself together. 'Courage,' he muttered to himself as he straightened his reefer jacket. 'I've lost my equanimity,' he thought wonderingly to himself. He took a deep breath, his cap from the hook and headed for the bridge. Oddly he found himself thinking of Gwendolen, and when he touched the engine room telegraphs his hands were quite steady again.

Stanier nursed a feeling of quiet content-ment after his victory. For the first time since arriving in Porth Ardur he felt he was a man who had his finger on the pulse, that his life was well-ordered and successful and that his future prospects were good. He put into his preparations for the cruise all the enthusiasm that youth could muster. His seamen were recruited and on pay and the yacht was approaching a state of maintained perfection that even the most demanding Master in the I&O would approve of.

His affair with Tegwyn was outwardly discreet and privately abandoned, which suited his own particular demands. As far as Stanier was concerned there was no cooling in his ardour, yet an astute observer, had there been one, might have detected a regularity occurring in the couple's sexual activity which was the precursor of a lowering in temperature.

As far as Tegwyn was concerned, Stanier was becoming an obsession in her life. She had never met a man who outwardly showed a woman such attention, who acted with such gallantry and yet in private demanded and delighted her. Used as she was to the hot passion of Celtic manhood, where ardour was everything and privacy irrelevant, Tegwyn felt like a duchess. She was also ravished by the prospect of the cruise in the *Sea Dragon* and was happily aware of having stimulated a certain amount of disapproving jealousy among the other women of Porth Ardur.

Tegwyn Morgan would never have passed so far down the path of moral disintegration had her mother been unpreoccupied. Justine lived in a rosy glow of anticipation. She saw Macready only once a week as she had always done, yet felt no pang of jealousy when he was home with his wife. For years Justine had nurtured her secret, unnameable passion for her dead husband. It was not difficult for her to fantasise over the Captain and even, in moments of rare and delicious delight, over both of them.

Her whole voluptuous frame seemed to ripen during those summer weeks so that she resembled a fruit at the very fullness of its promise, an instant before it fell from the tree, to bruise and wither upon the ground.

Caryatid plunged into a grey swell, pushing her bow into it, thrusting and rising as she lifted to it. A patter of spray came aboard and the white water of her wake hissed away on either bow. 'There must have been a blow somewhere to the westward,' offered Charlie to no one in particular.

'M'mmm,' agreed Bernard Foster, staring through his glasses and still wondering what Stanier had said to upset Captain Macready.

'Look, Charlie,' he said suddenly. Charlie picked up the telescope and levelled it to the north.

Caryatid was steaming slowly west, along the line of the Hellweather Bank. The sandbank ran for eleven miles roughly east to west and was about two miles wide at its greatest breadth. At its western end the lightvessel of the same name bobbed up and down, its red hull defaced by the huge black and white letters that told mariners totally ignorant of their position where they were. A mile east of the lightvessel and on the very tip of the shoaling water the West Hellweather Buoy was situated. Or it should have been. On this occasion it appeared to have parted its chain mooring and driven ashore onto the bank. Bernard

175

Foster had seen it, a red and white can lying on its side on the top of an exposed section of the shoal.

He blew down the voice-pipe and Captain Macready came up to the bridge. The ship was stopped and the three men stared to the north while the quartermaster idly spun the spokes of the wheel, privately betting whether or not the Old Man would go in and get the stranded buoy.

Charlie suffered a sinking feeling in his stomach as he looked across at the buoy. There was a light westerly wind and the sky had become overcast. The day was not greatly inspiring. But to the north of them the sea seemed to lift and heave as the swells hunched up and flung themselves thunderously at the impeding sand bank. Suddenly the name Hellweather seemed horribly apt. The exposed sand was only visible now and then, around it white water and spray foamed and dissipated its latent energy in a roar that was audible to the three observers over half a mile away. At last Macready spoke.

'It's an ebb tide. We'll lay the new buoy

then steam in from the other side. It may be possible to get a boat in on the lee side of the bank. Alright, Mr Farthing?'

'Aye, aye, sir,' said Charlie, suddenly realising why seamen never used the word 'Yes.'

An hour and a half later, the new buoy was laid at the West Hellweather station and *Caryatid* steamed away from it. The gleaming, unweathered newness of its paint made it a bright jewelled spot against the grey back-cloth of sea and sky.

The spot got smaller and smaller and Charlie was aware of a quivering feeling in his stomach. It increased when he noticed the seamen congregating around the motor boat. Bernard Foster was earnestly giving the coxswain some instructions and momentarily Charlie resented the implied lack of faith in his own judgement. Then the butterflies reasserted their presence in his stomach and he acknowledged the wisdom of the Mate.

Foster came forward.

'I've just had a word with Mackerel Jack, Charlie. He's the best boat handler in the ship, you can rely on him, okay?'

Charlie nodded. 'What's the urgency to get this damaged buoy back?'

'They don't often break adrift. We ought to know why. Besides it won't stay there, it'll probably drift off and float about to the confusion of all, a danger to navigation.' He smiled reassuringly and added in a lower voice in which there was just a hint of pride, 'Besides, we don't like losing them, it's a bad advertisement.'

Charlie looked back at the *Caryatid* as the motor boat chugged away. Her low freeboard disappeared behind a swell, leaving only her bridge, masts and funnel visible. She reappeared on the crest, her straight, workmanlike stem looked incongruous compared with her elegant counter and he found himself smiling, admiring the plucky little ship that went about its difficult business without fuss. He looked into the well of the boat where an enormous coil of three and a half inch manila hemp had been carefully coiled. The bowman, muffled in black oilskins and sou'wester, his stocky frame augmented by a life jacket, whistled softly to himself. The coxswain stood at the tiller, the only man compelled to stare ahead.

As the boat approached, Charlie saw the buoy. The tide had ebbed considerably and a fairly large area of sand was exposed. Beyond the buoy the swells thundered eight or nine feet in the air as they reared up, toppled and broke upon the sand in a thunder that drowned the boat's engine. On this side of the bank, however, the effect was broken. The swells rolled along, suddenly covering and then exposing the sand as trough succeeded crest. There were no breakers and Charlie heaved a sigh of relief. But it was short-lived, for the rise and fall remained significant. He was aware that the bowman had grabbed the boat hook and was stabbing downwards as the boat fell into a trough. He was periodically looking aft and shaking his head. The third member of the boat's crew was busy aft and as soon as the bowman nodded that he had a sounding, an anchor flashed overboard and a grass line snaked after it.

Charlie felt redundant and bit his lip.

Suddenly the boat bumped hard, the whole of her keel slamming down on the rock-hard, impacted sand. There was a shout from aft as Mackerel Jack gunned the engine into reverse while the third seaman quickly recovered the anchor warp to avoid fouling the propeller.

'I can get no further, Mr Farthing,' Mackerel yelled at Charlie. That much was obvious. There was an instant's pregnant silence while the boat's crew waited for their officer to make his executive decision.

'Shit!' thought Charlie. Then stung into action by his impotence he grabbed the manila line, put a bowline in it and slipped the bight over one shoulder.

'I'll go,' he yelled. 'When I've gone, back her off a bit.' Then in a quieter voice to the bowman, 'Pay the line out.' He jumped over the side.

Despite the season the water's chill shocked him. It came up to his chest and he floundered, dignity disappearing as he saw the grin on the bowman's face. That worthy had assumed he would be ordered into the water and had been contemplating how one disobeyed an order given by Mr Farthing.

Charlie suddenly felt the swell lift him. His lifejacket buoyed him up and he kicked out his legs, rolling onto his back. He was already twenty feet from the boat. He thrashed out, feeling the drag of the rope, kicking with single-mindedness. He looked up at the grey wrack in the sky and thought of Sonia. He kicked harder until suddenly he felt a swell depart and he grounded flat on his back, a large untidy seal.

He stood up on water-logged sand. His sweater and serge trousers dripped water and both socks had come off.

Waving at the boat he pulled in some slack rope then trudged across to the buoy, the sand sucking at his feet. The base of the buoy was towards him, weed-encrusted like a great hairy mollusc. Charlie saw at once what had happened. No chain was attached to the buoy for the lug to which it was secured, the arse-iron as it was called, had fractured. He dragged a bight of rope round to the other end of the buoy and secured the rope to the nose iron. The topmark and staff were missing. Pulling all the slack rope with him he turned back towards the boat.

Mackerel edged the boat in and the bowman pulled the rope as tight as he could so that Charlie half swam, half hauled himself back out to the boat. With a great effort the seamen dragged him dripping aboard.

'You must be fuckin' freezin', Sec,' said the bowman matter-of-factly. Charlie grinned. He no longer felt such a beginner.

Mackerel backed off into deeper water and turned the boat. The anchor warp was transferred to the bow and the manila snaked out over the transom as he edged back to his anchor. A few grunting jerks and it came home.

The motor launch chugged slowly back towards *Caryatid*.

The steamer had come close in now and anchored. Charlie could see she was in shallow water as her roll was exaggerated. He looked anxiously at the length of rope remaining in the boat and the distance still to go. But Bernard Foster was far too careful a man to be caught on that score, and there were still ten fathoms in the boat when the end was passed up onto the *Caryatid*'s foredeck.

'That's most extraordinary, Mr Farthing,' said Captain Macready, looking Charlie up and down.

'Sorry, sir?' said the younger man, uncomprehending.

'Your clothes are soaking wet, yet your seaboots are comparatively dry,' Captain Macready was smiling.

Charlie laughed. 'Oh I never swim in my boots, sir.'

'You'd better get dried off, Mr Farthing,' said Captain Macready who had almost recovered his composure. Except, of course, when he actually thought of Stanier.

Stanier had a phonecall on the Friday morning to inform him that Sir Hector's party would arrive on Sunday night. He immediately set about the final preparation aboard *Sea Dragon*. His first priority was to turn her in her berth so that she could be steamed out of the inner harbour with the least possible fuss and the maximum panache.

During this operation the dock gates were opened for several fishing boats as it was within half an hour of high water. Across the dock Thomas Jones put down the telephone receiver and tossed off his mug of tea.

'*Carry*'ll be here in about an hour,' he said to Stan who nodded. Jones looked out of the window.

'Stupid bastard still fiddlin' with that yacht, Tom?' asked Stan.

Jones nodded. 'Be bloody glad to see the back of 'im next week.'

'What'll we do without 'im?' demanded Stan in mock horror.

'Fuckin' manage, that's what!' volunteered Fred, speaking for the first time, unable to stand the philosophical attitude of his colleagues. 'He's a pain in the bloody arse.'

'Now Fred, calm down, he won't be here long.'

'How d'you work that out?' asked Fred

sharply, immediately interested.

Jones shrugged. 'Stands to reason, see. Man like Stanier's too ambitious for the likes of Port'Ardur. You watch this connection with Sir Bloody Hector.'

Jones turned away from the window and sat down. Fred got out a pack of cards.

Stanier completed mooring *Sea Dragon* and left her. High water had already passed and he noticed with annoyance that the caisson gates were still open. Of 'his staff' there was no sign. He walked along the quay to the lock head opposite to his brick caboose. Between him and his office yawned the offending gap. An apple core was moving slowly, almost imperceptibly out. He raised his voice and shouted.

'Office 'hoy!' There was no response.

Stanier flushed with annoyance. 'Jones!' he roared in the sort of bellow that one expects from annoyed Master Mariners.

'Raise you,' said Jones, 'who's makin' that bleedin' noise?'

'Stanier,' said Fred not looking up but staring gloomily at his hand.

'Shit!' said Jones getting up and laying a

royal flush on the table. He went outside.

'Jones! What the hell are you playing at?' Stanier yelled across the entrance, ignoring the dozen or so loungers, rod fishermen and holiday-makers that turned, attracted by the Harbour Master's bawling.

'Sorry, Cap'n? What's up?' Jones was deliberately dense. Fred and Stan came out behind him. Fred said, *Carry*'s coming up the bay.'

'What's up?' yelled Stanier. 'It's well after high water, that's what's up. How many times do I have to tell you that I want the dock impounded on top of the tide and this is the best tide this month and the bloody ebb's away! Well, don't just stand there, man. Close the damned gates!'

'Close the gates, Cap'n?' hedged Jones, aware that Stanier was a comfortable distance from him while they remained open.

'Yes damn it, close them!'

'But the *Car*—'

'Don't argue! Close the damned gates!' Stanier was practically beside himself, well aware that he was not coming off best and that there were nearly two dozen onlookers now, if one excepted the faces at the windows of The Feathers.

'Oh, fuck it,' said Fred, striding over to the lever that controlled the gates.

'But Fred ... ' began Jones then shrugged. As Fred said, 'Fuck it.'

As the gates began to close, Stanier moved out along the catwalk so that when they met he strode rapidly across to where his staff stood. It was like Napoleon admonishing his marshals.

'We're pushing it a bit, sir,' said Foster to Captain Macready. Macready lowered his binoculars. 'But we're alright,' he said reassuringly. 'I've asked the chief for maximum full speed until I ring down.'

Foster nodded. 'I'll get the hands to stand-by then?'

'Very well, Mr Foster.' Captain Macready raised his glasses again just to confirm matters.

Caryatid steamed up the bay, smoke

belching from her funnel and a great bone in her teeth. The hands came up and lounged on the rail as they watched draw near the dear, familiar roofs of Porth Ardur nestling under the shadow of Mynydd Uchaf.

'He's in a hurry,' said Chippy spitting over the rail.

'Ebb's away, Chips,' said the Bosun knowledgeably, 'and there's dancin' to-night.'

Captain Macready rang 'Stop engines' just off the end of the mole. *Caryatid* slowed. 'Hard a-port!' he snapped and the steamer began to turn, slowing all the while. As she opened up the dock entrance Macready swore. The gates were closed against him. Simultaneously the quartermaster shouted, 'Gates are closed, sir!'

'Midships ... steady.' Macready put out his hand to yank the telegraphs to full astern. Instinctively he looked aft, anxiously noting that *Caryatid* was still moving quite rapidly ahead. Then he saw something that changed his mind.

'Steady up for the centre of the gates, quartermaster.'

There was a silence then: 'Steady for the centre of the gates, sir.'

'Thank you.' Macready felt quite light-headed. He quickly scanned the mole for Jones or his side kicks but then caught sight of them standing in a knot with Stanier. He rang 'Slow astern' dragging some of the way off *Caryatid*. On the foredeck anxious faces, Foster's among them, stared uncomprehendingly up at the bridge. The Mate started to come aft, remembering the strange mood he had found the Captain in earlier in the week.

'Have two fenders ready, Mr Foster,' said Macready in a clear voice and the Mate turned forward. Macready rang the engines to 'Stop.'

On the mole Stanier's diatribe was never finished. It faded out as he realised that his three underlings were looking intently behind him. Something of very great interest was obviously distracting them. He turned round.

Caryatid was about fifty feet from the

gates, creeping inexorably ahead. Stanier rushed forward onto the catwalk over the tops of the gates. One hand was raised like a policeman.

'It's past high water! The port's closed! You'll damage the gates! Go astern!' As he issued each of these peremptory instructions his voice rose so that by the last, already weakened by too much shouting, it cracked into a squeak.

There were now about forty people standing on the quay.

Stanier reached the centre of the gates at the precise instant that *Caryatid*'s stem touched them.

'Wouldn't crack a fuckin' egg,' opined the seaman holding one hand fender over the starboard bow.

'Fuckin' beautiful,' agreed the seaman holding a hand fender over the port bow. Beneath them Stanier looked up. Foster looked over, then embarrassed, he looked away again.

Stanier was aware that his nose was about twelve inches from the sheer black bar of *Caryatid*'s stem. Some agency was

190

easing his legs apart with a far from erotic sensation. He looked down. A gap of water showed between them. *Caryatid* was forcing the gates gently open. Stanier realised he had a foot on each caisson and that if he did not do something very quickly, he was going to fall into the dock. His decision was prompted more by an instinct for survival than by common sense, for the side he ended up on was that from which he had started some twenty minutes earlier.

As soon as Jones saw Stanier safe he flung over the lever and opened the gates

'Like fuckin' rape,' said the seaman on the starboard bow, hauling his redundant fender inboard.

'Fuckin' beautiful,' agreed his companion on the port bow.

Caryatid eased into her berth and Captain Macready rang 'Finished with engines'. He was just descending from the bridge when an anxious Bernard Foster appeared.

'Harbour Master to see you, sir.'

Stanier pushed past Foster. He was red

with fury at his public humiliation. Not only had he been made to look a fool, he had been compelled to walk the entire circuit of the dock, past his own grinning crew aboard *Sea Dragon* and a crowd that was beginning to attract attention itself, as crowds have a habit of doing.

'What the bloody hell kind of a display of seamanship do you call *that*, Macready!?' Stanier roared, practically foaming at the mouth. 'You bloody stupid, incompetent fool!'

Macready smiled. 'Would you mind stepping out on the boat deck a moment, Harbour Master?' The Captain of the *Caryatid* gestured Stanier to the teak door.

Stanier stumbled over the high coaming. 'What the goddamned—?'

Macready followed him and gently pushed him round clear of the funnel ventilators. With the utmost gravity Macready raised his arm and pointed,

It was a gesture pregnant with confidence.

Stanier looked. Against the blue hills on the far side of the bay the end of the mole stood out. Rising from its extremity the signal mast and yard bore four black balls disposed in a square.

'The port's open, Harbour Master, you forgot to take down the signals ...'

The Cruise of the Sea Dragon

Sir Hector's domestic staff arrived on Saturday evening. The knight bachelor and his guests were due for dinner the following evening. The meal was to be an informal buffet to which James Stanier and 'lady' were cordially invited. Stanier was not a man to be outdone in matters of protocol. He and Tegwyn had arranged that he should meet Sir Hector and his party and that she should arrive herself some ten minutes later.

Stanier was well satisfied with *Sea Dragon*. Her teak decks were spotlessly clean and all paint drops had been carefully scraped off. The white paint was pristine and the teak rails, doors and other brightwork shone with the incomparable sheen of fresh copal varnish. All visible brass was polished and Stanier himself had made some fancy rope-work in white cotton line for the accommodation ladder, learnt on his training ship a decade earlier. He had had the anchor crowns picked out in blue and the cable lengths over the toy windlass enamelled in white. All parcelling was finished at either end with four-strand turks' heads and any rope's end about the deck was cheesed. Captain Stanier was justifiably pleased with the appearance of his first command.

There was only one cloud on the horizon. He had been unable to purchase a mess jacket in Porth Ardur and, as Master of the *Sea Dragon,* did not wish to resort to a dinner jacket when dining with Sir Hector and his friends. However he had hit upon the expedient of dispatching Fred into the nearest major town, some thirty miles away, where telephoned enquiries had elicited the information that such items might be purchased.

Fred was expected back at any time and before proceeding ashore to his house Stanier had gone below to consult Sir Hector's steward on the identity of the expected guests.

He found the steward, who was a butler ashore. 'Good evening, Horrocks, isn't it?'

Horrocks was a small, neat, competent man. 'Yes sir, that is correct.'

'Well, Horrocks, could you tell me exactly who to expect tomorrow?'

'Certainly, sir. Apart of course from Sir Hector there will be his associate, Mr Argyle. Mr Argyle is a ship-broker, sir, and will probably bring his secretary who is usually a Miss Dorothy Loring ...' Irony was absent from Horrock's voice, though the merest inflection on the words carried a conviction more potent than crude explanation. '... I expect Mr Pomeroy will be of the party, he's an extremely wealthy young man who has invested heavily in Sir Hector's shipping company.'

'And Mr Pomeroy's lady?' asked Stanier.

'I doubt it, sir. I do not believe there *is* a Mrs Pomeroy. Mr Pomeroy prefers to travel alone, sir. Mr Pomeroy is an Old Etonian, sir, and a former Guards officer.'

'I see,' said Stanier. 'Anyone else?'

Horrocks shrugged. 'It is possible Miss

Caroline may come, sir, she is a somewhat impulsive young woman...'

'Miss Caroline?'

'Sir Hector's daughter, sir.'

'I was unaware that Sir Hector was married ...'

'Sir Hector and Lady Blackadder are estranged, sir,' explained Horrocks, in a tone that precluded further enquiries.

Fred resented his mission to such an extent that he got no further than the Station Bar, where he got so drunk that he missed the train. It was fortunate that in staggering home he met Jones who, quickly discovering that Fred had failed to collect Stanier's mess kit, was prescient enough to realise a contingency plan was required.

Jones left Fred to his fate and, mounting his bicycle, swiftly descended the hill to the harbour. He met Mackerel Jack at the gangway of *Caryatid*. Mackerel had the watch and was also known to Jones. The two men retired to the messroom for a conference on terms and when it was concluded, in the currency of pints of beer ultimately chargeable to Fred, they proceeded into the officers' accommodation.

The conspirators' biggest problem was the presence of Second Officer Charles Farthing, but they discovered him dozing on his settee and moved swiftly past his cabin door.

It was the work of a few minutes to slip the latch in the Captain's door and enter Macready's cabin. Twenty minutes after boarding *Caryatid* Thomas Jones was ashore again, cycling round to *Sea Dragon* with a bundle under his arm.

'Don't forget to square it with the steward,' were his last words to Mackerel Jack.

'Don't forget the bloody beer,' replied the seaman.

'So you'll be away next weekend, dear?' asked Gwendolen Macready.

'Er, yes, we've the big job to do at Ynyscraven and I don't anticipate finishing it before the following Monday ... There, does that look better?' Macready stepped back and lowered paint pot and brush to the floor.

'Yes, that's very nice. Right then, I'll have the vicar organise the PCC meeting here, that'll ease the burden on his wife, she's not been at all well lately, d'you know Septimus ...' But Septimus did not know, neither did he honestly care, he just kept thinking of Justine.

'There love, that's the best I can do for you.' Justine tied the ribbon around the cardboard box. 'Alright Betty, I'll lock up, hang on a minute, love ...'

Betty Byford said her 'Goodnight, see you on Monday,' and left the shop. Tegwyn waited impatiently for her mother.

'I know you're itching to be off, dear, but I would be stupid if I didn't know the purpose of some of the things in there.'

Justine indicated the box under Tegwyn's arm. The little shop was stuffy. Motes danced in the slanting rays of late afternoon sunshine that poured in through its one window. Tegwyn tightened her arm possessively around the box. It contained a frothy confection of lingerie that she had not known her mother stocked. She flushed, feeling her cheeks burn.

'Are you sleeping with him, love?' asked Justine, realising that she had paid scant attention to her daughter in recent weeks and knowing the answer to her question before she asked it. Tegwyn was silent.

'Of course you are ... well, don't say I didn't warn you about him when he drops you, and don't think I approve because I don't but I can't condemn you and don't want you hurt, love.' Justine gently took the box from her daughter and laid it on the counter.

'You just be careful, my girl.' She said the words in that low husky voice that men privileged to hear, never forgot. The two women looked at each other. Tears of happiness were welling in Tegwyn's eyes, tears of compassion in her mother's. The two clasped together, then Justine kissed her daughter's mouth and drew away. Tegwyn was very lovely. For the first time Justine experienced a real pang of painful jealousy: she envied her daughter's flesh, even the faint, betraying shadows beneath her eyes. Tegwyn submitted herself proudly to Justine's gaze. She had lost that slightly inferior feeling when in the very physical presence of her mother.

'Goodbye, Mother.'

'Goodbye, *cariad.*' Justine turned away. She felt like a relay runner who had just handed over the baton. There was nothing further for her but to slow down and pull off the track.

Captain James St John Stanier watched the Daimler pull up ('The car's nothing pretentious, old boy,' he could hear Sir Hector say). The chauffeur jumped out and opened the doors. From the back Sir Hector emerged followed by a small, stocky, grey-haired man of about fifty, presumably Argyle, thought Stanier. The stocky man handed out a youngish woman, little taller than himself, with dark hair and a compact figure.

'Miss Loring,' explained a voice at his elbow. Stanier turned to find Horrocks. He nodded. Next out was a graceful blonde

201

of about thirty who tossed her hair as she straightened up.

'Sir Hector's special guest, sir,' said the *sotto voce* Horrocks. 'I omitted to inform you earlier as one is never quite sure ...' a gentle, dignified emphasis lay on the words 'special' and 'quite'.

'That's Mr Pomeroy.'

Stanier looked at a foppish young man coming round the bonnet of the car.

'No Miss Caroline?'

'Not as yet, sir.'

Sir Hector led them on board and made introductions.

Tegwyn arrived some twenty minutes later in a taxi. For Tegwyn to travel in a taxi was something of a treat but it was a comment on her self-confidence that she alighted from it as though the occurrence was not unusual. She was fortunate in having acquired a deportment peculiar to duchesses or exceptional dancers. Stanier was at the gangway to meet her. Any misgivings he might have had at her appearance were instantly dispelled, for she managed the gangway without those irritatingly superfluous giggles that women often use at such moments.

Neither was her Ardurian accent out of place when Stanier introduced her, for Argyle's Gaelic burr was matched by Miss Loring's unmistakable Cockney. The only person who showed any inclination to be stand-offish was Sir Hector's special guest, who was introduced as Samantha.

As Stanier relaxed with his third whisky he looked happily around. Things were going very well, very well indeed.

Charlie Farthing saw the lights in *Sea Dragon*'s saloon. He slipped up to the bridge of the *Caryatid* and focused the long glass on the windows. Charlie was bored, impatient and longing for Monday when *Caryatid* would head for Ynyscraven.

He was even more impatient when he at last took the glass from his eye, for the sight of laughing women and the lights catching the gentle swellings of silk covered breasts was having an effect upon his pulse rate.

It was even worse later. He had tried to turn in early but constant thoughts of Sonia, not all of them of the purest, had driven him out on deck to pace up and down. Here he had been subjected to the mirth of post-prandial diners taking their brandy on *Sea Dragon*'s open quarterdeck.

In the end Charlie gave up and went off to The Feathers, where he found Calico Jack. Rank was abolished and the two got drunk together, happily telling their most intimate secrets to each other until it began to dawn on Charlie that here, if Calico had his way, was his prospective father-in-law.

Sea Dragon sailed from Porth Ardur shortly before noon on the Monday morning. Her departure was watched by *Caryatid*'s crew who paused in the operation of taking on board the long five-inch wire for the lighthouse hoist.

Sir Hector and Argyle were sitting in the smoke room reading the papers but Pomeroy and the ladies were out on the quarterdeck, their hair rippled by the sea breeze and cardigans loosely about their shoulders.

There were one or two ribald remarks from *Caryatid*'s foredeck and a clenched fist was jerked in an obscene gesture which elicited a guffaw of laughter from the seamen, but Stanier did nothing to bring on his head the disapprobation of the watching 'experts'.

The woman called Samantha turned to Pomeroy and in a coolly arch voice asked 'I expect you'd rather be over there amongst all those sailors, wouldn't you, darling?'

Tegwyn, only half aware that there was something different about the young man, turned to catch his reply.

'Only if you're going to be beastly for the whole trip, Sammy, then I'd rather.'

'I expect you'll find something to tickle your Greek fancy ...'

Pomeroy ignored her and smiled at Tegwyn. 'I must say,' he said, 'that crepe-de-chine blouse suits you admirably, Miss Morgan.' He touched her arm. The gesture was one of extreme delicacy. Involuntarily,

Tegwyn shuddered with pleasure. Pomeroy smiled again.

On her back in the heather Sonia stared skywards. The blue arch of the sky soared above her. No cloud was visible and she tried unsuccessfully to grasp what she was looking at. It was infinity, blue infinity and yet it was nothing, nothing at all.

She sighed languorously. The sky, the hugeness of it was like love ... she fought off clichés which seemed to cheapen the sensation of being at one with that blueness. She felt the ground warm beneath her and breathed deeply, pressing the palms of her hands onto the roughness of the heather. Her breasts rose and fell in slow undulations.

She thought about Charlie and suddenly realised that all the time her subconscious was debating whether or not she would let him make love to her. Her breathing quickened and she opened her legs a little, trying hard to imagine what it was like ...

A shadow fell suddenly across her

face. She sat up guiltily, flushing at being discovered with her mind in such abandoned raptures and imagining her fantasy was written in letters upon her forehead. The kestrel, hovering between Sonia and the sun, side-slipped at the sudden movement.

Sonia clasped her knees and transferred her gaze to the sea. It stretched empty to the horizon. No, a small white dot was away to the north east. She lay back again. Small white dots were not the *Caryatid*.

Presently she rose. The light breeze that blew up on the spine of Ynyscraven moulded her blouse around her. Her nipples stood out, rigid against the material. The white speck that Sonia had seen was the westward steaming *Sea Dragon*.

The *Sea Dragon*'s cruise, like any voyage, soon settled down to a daily routine in which all aboard participated to a greater or lesser degree. Breakfast was not compulsory but Sir Hector expected all his guests to be present for morning coffee at which the social events of the day were discussed.

They might land on an island or at a fishing village, anchor to sunbathe and swim, or steam as close inshore as Stanier dared, which was not very close since he was trained to keep a good offing.

The weather was kind. Day after day of light breezes and sunshine prevailed. Indolence and pleasure sailed with the passengers of the *Sea Dragon* against the deceptively picturesque backdrop of the Cambrian coast.

The party, which considered itself the ultimate in civilised sophistication during the day, occupied itself at night according to its inclinations. Sir Hector, a man of easy morals, was not a degenerate and although it was obvious that carnal liaisons were the main purpose of the cruise, they were required to be discreet.

Private opinions tended to be concealed and the party rubbed along without friction in an atmosphere in which the food, the wine, the weather and the delightful prospect of the seascape tended to enervate the participants. Even the arrival of Miss Caroline failed to upset the delicate balance of the yacht's ethos.

Miss Caroline joined when *Sea Dragon* put into a small port about fifty miles west of Porth Ardur. She was slender with bobbed hair and an air of restless energy that must have characterised her father at an earlier age. She was also slightly loud in her opinions and this might have ruined the equanimity of the party had she not been dropped by her latest boyfriend but a day earlier. This circumstance tended to render her less disruptive, and she fell into deep, meaningful silences that the others thankfully ignored.

To some extent, however, her presence was a problem. All the other members of the group had selected, and tacitly acknowledged, their sexual partners. Now Caroline by herself threatened to upset the equilibrium.

The party had devised a little ritual after dinner in which the partners left the company. The pecking order had been established the first night when Stanier had been aware of his responsibilities.

At about eleven o'clock he had excused

himself: 'Perhaps you would excuse me? I have to write up my night orders.' Goodnights were exchanged and then, 'Tegwyn, would you care to see the view from the bridge?' at which hint the two left. The others then stretched or drained their glasses or filled them for a night-cap, and the party dispersed.

When, the following night, the hour had approached eleven, Sir Hector had said, 'I suppose, Captain, you have to write up your orders?' Stanier took the hint and the ritual was established.

But Caroline did not interfere with the arrangements, at least not at this juncture, for her self-esteem was undergoing an extensive rebuilding programme from which, her father privately assured Argyle, she would presently bounce back with disarming force.

Stanier was enjoying himself. It must be admitted he took to his job like a duck to water. If he erred on the side of caution his confidence increased daily until at the end of the first week his self-esteem had reached a new peak. His professionalism reasserted itself as the mainspring of his life and his interest in Tegwyn began its inevitable wane. There were other thoughts in his head besides the management of *Sea Dragon*. His spell as commander of the yacht brought realisation of the limitations of his post at Porth Ardur. In private conversation Sir Hector had repeatedly intimated an interest in Stanier's career that was fast becoming paternal. Argyle, a shrewd Gael, had quizzed him several. times and given Stanier the impression he was undergoing an examination rather than an interview.

Finally Stanier was attracted by the person of Caroline, whose languid attitudes about the decks of *Sea Dragon* were a sharp contrast to Tegwyn's more obsessive nature. Stanier had enjoyed almost every one of his adolescent fantasies in actuality with Tegwyn. He had worked through the gamut of his imaginative lusts and it was beginning to dawn, at least on his subconscious, that he was drowning in the flesh of Tegwyn Morgan. By contrast Caroline was enigmatic and distant. She was also slightly romantic, at least to the pragmatic judgement of James St John Stanier.

After all, her father was an extremely wealthy man.

Poor Tegwyn was quite unaware of the gradual cooling of her lover. Every night with the faithful loyalty of the true mistress she adorned her body for him. Her allurements were always irresistible and she gave him physical love with an enthusiasm that could only come from a devotion that transcended the carnal.

So besotted had she become, and so romantic were her circumstances aboard *Sea Dragon,* that her happiness was undisturbed when Stanier came down late to her cabin. She believed his excuse that he had thought the yacht might be dragging her anchor and had found it necessary to check the position.

She did not know that Caroline had begun to bounce back.

Stanier had been en route to Tegwyn's

cabin as was his usual practice when a figure waylaid him from the shadow of the engine room ventilator.

'Good evening, Caroline,' he had said, instantly recognising the girl since the moon was full and shone from a sky devoid of even a wisp of cloud.

'Good evening, Captain. It's a beautiful night.'

'Yes indeed. I wish you wouldn't be so formal. My name's James.'

'Would you be offended if I called you Jimmy?' Stanier detested the idea but found himself saying, 'Of course not.'

She moved over to the rail then leaning back on it, faced him.

'My father's interested in you. Says you've a ruthless streak. I should say he was probably considering taking you for a partner. He's acutely conscious that he's already outlived his own father. I was supposed to be a son.' She turned and gazed out over the moonlit sea. The lights of a little town were going out one by one. The mountains rising behind looked as they might have done a millennium earlier.

'Come here beside me, Jimmy.' He moved over and leant beside her.

'I expect that he will be planning how to get you and me together. As you are, at present, occupied you'll get an invitation to Laycocks, that's our house. Probably for Christmas if not before.'

Stanier was stunned into silence.

'Haven't you anything to say, Jimmy?'

Stanier shook his head. 'Not really, I'm a little dazed, that's all ...' Pictures of Stanier as a successful ship-owner swam into his imagination.

'You'll be expected to marry me, of course, having done a voyage in command of one of Daddy's ships.'

Stanier's heart leapt. Then he could really call himself 'Captain' and perhaps, or was this going too far, perhaps there might yet be a knighthood?

He looked sideways at Caroline. Marriage?

She turned and looked back at him.

'Well?'

'D'*you* want to marry me, Caroline?'

She smiled, a cold, resolved, Saxon smile.

'As you were gentleman enough to ask me I'll give it my consideration. Good night, Captain.'

The result of this conversation made no difference to the behaviour of either Stanier or Caroline. She waited on events and he waited for her reply, wondering whether he had made a fool of himself, or whether, quite by accident, he might be on the verge of a successful liaison. In the meantime he continued to satisfy Tegwyn, such is the fecundity of youth. It was almost a week after their departure from Porth Ardur when Sir Hector suggested a visit to Ynyscraven. *Sea Dragon* was well to the westward and it was late on Sunday evening when the blue painted anchor dropped from her gleaming bow.

She shared the anchorage with the steam vessel *Caryatid*.

The Ravens of Dungarth

The island of Ynyscraven lies in the Silurian Strait like a giant, elongated 'Q'. Millions of years before man's antecedents emerged from the primeval slime, geological changes had wrought it of a hump of granite with a covering of oil-bearing shale. Most of the shale had weathered away except at the southern end of the island. The northern extremity was high and fairly steep-to, a broken escarpment plunging into the sea and giving the lighthouse a tiny plateau to cling to. Thousands of screaming sea-birds, from auks to shags, nested here.

The higher spine of the island was mainly covered with heather or bracken, though areas of grass and gorse provided rough pasture for sheep and the hardy ponies that constituted the island's most prestigious 'export'.

The land sloped slightly to the settled southern end where, with the granite disappearing under the more dramatically eroded shale, it became an untidy victim to the ravages of the Atlantic. Here the tail of the 'Q' extended south and east in a long vicious reef that at low water had the appearance of a row of slavering fangs as the ocean sucked and swirled white about them.

This reef was appropriately known as the Hound's Teeth and although dangerous, for the tide set across the jumble of rocks on both ebb and flood, its presence formed a lagoon-like anchorage within which ships of a considerable tonnage could lie in comfort and ride out any gales that blew from the prevailing wind directions of south-west to north-west. At the easternmost extremity of the reef, where Ynyscraven finally gave up its struggle with the sea and fell away to deep water, a bell buoy clanged its dolorous warning.

The noise of the Hound Buoy was the first indication to Justine that she was nearing the island. Despite the relative calm of the sea, the fishing vessel *Plover* was scarcely the *Mauretania* and Justine's passage from Aberogg had been decidedly uncomfortable. It had not been helped by the fact that she had not eaten for many hours. So excited was she that the thought of stopping to consume food was repugnant to her. Almost as soon as Tegwyn had left the shop and long before *Caryatid* had even had steam raised in her boilers, Justine had reached the station and taken a train on her circuitous route to Aberogg.

The *Plover* was on a fortnightly contract to take mail and provisions to the island and bring off sheep, ponies and passengers. There were no cabins for the latter, who had to take pot luck in the tiny messroom with such of the three crew who happened to be below. Justine's imposing appearance and friendly manner had of course charmed the three fishermen, who offered her every comfort their little ship could muster.

Nevertheless she was thankful when the *Plover* rubbed alongside the tiny stone jetty and she could take her trembling limbs ashore. The *Plover*'s skipper deputed his 'boy', a fair giant of about twenty-five, to shoulder her suitcase and walk up the steep path to the reeve's house.

Justine was utterly enchanted with the house in its little coombe. A small, neat lawn was overhung by trees that sheltered in the diminutive valley, and the smell of soft earth and flowers greeted her.

Inside the house she met the reeve and his wife. They appeared to be somewhat embarrassed at her arrival and for one awful moment Justine thought that the conspiracy had been uncovered.

'Mrs Morgan, how nice to meet you. I am-er-well, it is a little awkward-um—'

'Mrs Morgan, what my husband is trying to say is that only this morning we received a message from our son that he wished to see us urgently. Captain Macready mentioned to us that you were a friend of his and his wife's and we wished you to stay with us. As a result my husband has let the two guest cottages ...' The reeve's wife spread her hands, 'You see our problem.'

219

'Well in that case, perhaps I ought to return ...'

'Oh good heavens no!' continued the woman. 'What we wondered was whether you would consider ... well, whether you would mind looking after the house for us? You see, we've no idea what our son wants, except that it's important, neither do we like leaving the house empty as we've a daily maid, the daughter of one of our shepherds, she's a bit careless without supervision ...'

Justine was, under the circumstances, hardly likely to refuse.

'No, of course, I shall be delighted. I am flattered that you trust me ...'

The reeve's wife made a deprecating gesture. 'You are a friend of Captain Macready's; that alone is recommendation enough and now that we've met you, well ... the arrangement seems satisfactory.' They smiled at each other.

'Besides,' added the reeve, 'you can't run away from Ynyscraven, even if you wanted to.' They all laughed, Justine with genuine mirth.

So, for a little while, Justine Morgan became mistress of the island of Ynyscraven.

Justine did not expect to see either Macready or *Caryatid* until Monday evening at the earliest. She therefore had slightly less than twenty-four hours to settle in. After the reeve and his wife had left and she had made the acquaintance of the maid, a simple red-faced child called, inappropriately, Faith, Justine explored the house.

It was double fronted and slate roofed. On either side of the entrance hall large reception rooms were sparsely but elegantly furnished. The floors were of stained boards with rich Indian rugs upon them. In one room a wall of bookshelves dominated the room; the other was a dining room with a long mahogany table. The stairs led to a passage that went across the back of the house with three bedrooms opening off it. Each had a double bed, a chair and a washstand with basin and ewer.

At the rear of the house a jumble of

kitchen, outhouses and stables gave way to the sheer rise of the rock wall that terminated the little coombe, so that one might have stood not twenty feet from the back of the house and thrown a stone down one of the chimneys.

The coombe faced east, losing the heat of the day early and soon in shadow. As the cool of a summer evening began to steal across the patch of grass, Justine ventured forth to inspect her domain. She also thought she might see the anchorage from the end of the garden.

She discovered the wicket gate and passed through it, recognising the path up which she had followed the fisherman earlier in the day. Retracing her steps a few yards she discovered a vantage point from which the whole bay lay below her.

'Are you looking for the *Caryatid*?' The voice made her jump. She looked round. A girl in an Aran sweater with russet hair and green eyes was standing behind her. 'You made me jump!' laughed Justine, still surprised.

'Are you waiting for the *Caryatid?*' the girl persisted.

'Well yes, as it happens, I am.' It was useless pretending for she and Macready were bound to be seen together. The girl came and stood next to her.

'She's expected up at the north end of the island tomorrow.'

'Oh I see,' Justine felt inadequate; this girl, appearing out of nowhere, seemed omniscient. 'How do you know?'

'I was up at the lighthouse this afternoon. The keepers told me. Are you staying at the reeve's house?'

'Yes I am. Do you live on the island?'

'Yes. My name's Sonia.' The girl turned and extended her hand. The two women faced each other and Justine found herself thinking of Tegwyn. This girl, of an age with her daughter and nothing like as beautiful, seemed much less vulnerable. They shook hands awkwardly and Sonia asked, 'Are you in love with someone aboard the *Caryatid?*'

Justine laughed, flashing her teeth in a smile that caught up her interlocutor so that Sonia too laughed. 'What on earth makes you ask that?'

Sonia shrugged. 'Why else are you here?'

'For a holiday, perhaps?' suggested Justine.

'You are far too beautiful to be on holiday alone,' said the girl with a directness that Justine found disarming. 'Besides, I'll soon find out. I know everything that happens on Ynyscraven.' She looked wistfully northwards to where a spur of cliff formed a small headland.

Justine felt the chill of night approaching and shivered involuntarily. She was about to turn away when Sonia spoke again in a lower, more confidential tone.

'I too am waiting for the *Caryatid*.'

'Are you in love with someone on board?' Justine asked. The girl nodded.

'I suppose that makes us sort of sisters,' she replied.

Justine chuckled. For a second the two stood silently then Justine had an idea. 'As you know all about the island you'll know I'm alone.'

'In the reeve's house, yes, I know that.'

'Would you join me for something to eat?' Justine was suddenly ravenous after her self-imposed fast. 'You can tell me all about Ynyscraven, the real Ynyscraven. I don't want to feel like a visitor while I'm here.'

Sonia looked at the dark, ripe beauty of the older woman. Justine would never be that, she thought. 'Your hair is as black as a raven's wing,' she said suddenly.

Justine moved her hand in an involuntary gesture to her head.

'I wonder if that is significant ...' Sonia's words faded away as though she were contemplating some secret problem.

'Will you come to the house ... say in half an hour?'

'Of course. One never refuses regal invitations.' Sonia turned abruptly away, leaving Justine completely confused. The girl's remark about her hair had been odd enough. Was this last a piece of insolence? If so it had been delivered in a strangely level way. Justine turned and walked back to the house. Below her the anchorage submitted to the shadow of the night.

The maid Faith was dismissed as soon as she and Justine had organised a fire in the sitting-room grate, found a cold shoulder of lamb and a jug of cider. Justine lit the oil lamps, pulled up a chair to the warmth of the fire and waited for Sonia. Around her the cold granite of the house was so still that she could hear the blood rushing in her ears.

When Sonia arrived Justine carved the meat and the two women sat at a small polished table. The oil lamp caught the girl's green eyes and Justine was surprised at the sudden beauty they lent to her face.

'Do you always talk in riddles?' she asked at last.

'I'm sorry, I didn't know I did ... oh, you mean what I said about regal commands?'

'Yes, that, and something about the colour of my hair being significant.'

'It's not dyed, is it?' Sonia was sharply inquisitive. She repented instantly. 'I'm sorry, that must have sounded very rude but it wouldn't be significant if it was dyed.'

Justine was about to deny that it was, then realised that women who deny things with vehemence are often thought of as lying. She put down her knife and fork and put her hands up behind her head.

Her hair tumbled about her shoulders, the lamp catching the blue lights in it. 'There,' she said. 'Is that as black as your raven's wing?'

Sonia rose and came round the table. Her fingers scarcely touched the tumbled mass. 'Yes, it is,' she said, sitting down again.

Justine tossed her head and flicked her hair behind her shoulders.

'Now you tell me all about it.'

Sonia put down her knife and fork. 'It would be easy to tell you if I knew why you have come to Ynyscraven. You have come here to love someone, haven't you? I bet I know who it is. As the reeve's left you in the house alone I'll guess: you're a friend of Captain Macready, he and the reeve are very thick ... am I right?'

'Perhaps,' said Justine, colouring. 'Love seems much on your mind.'

'Yes. Would you mind if I came and asked you things; not now, perhaps, but later?'

'Have you no family?'

'Not really, my mother's a little distant.'

'If I can help, of course.' Justine replied, wondering what, in this enchanted place, constituted distance.

'Thank you. Now let me tell you about the island. It belongs to the Earl of Dungarth. The Earl traces his line back to the Conqueror and it is said that the first of them came here just after the Conquest. At that time the island was independent. It seems to have held off the Saxons, for it had a Celtic monastery and a king. The first Earl had had the island included in his fief by the King and came to take possession of it, but his landing was disputed down in the bay where you came ashore. There was a fight and the king of Ynyscraven died, but the invaders were driven off for a while. The next east wind brought them back again. This time, the story goes, the Earl approached the beach under full sail and the wind was a gale. The defenders were well back and confident that the Earl's ships would be dashed to pieces. But they reckoned without knowing the spirit of the Earl. He ordered all his warriors to lie down while he took the helm of his ship and his lieutenant the helm of the other. Sorry, am I boring you?'

'No, my dear, I am fascinated. You mean all this happened just below where we were this afternoon?'

Sonia nodded, lowering her glass of cider. 'Well, the two ships drove straight up the beach, broached-to in the breakers, and as they rolled over, the Earl led his warriors ashore. The islanders were broken and fled, only a few remaining in the king's hall which was supposed to have been on the site of this house.

'The king had a queen who was a great beauty, a woman celebrated by poets for her raven hair, whose reputation is supposed to have inflamed the Earl and led to him begging the island as part of his

229

fief from the Conqueror in the first place, and also, of course, sharpening his desire to capture the island. She retired to an old hill fort, or dun, up on the high ground. It's near the lighthouse and you can still see the remains of it today. It's on a bit of a headland, or garth. It was called the 'fort on the point' or Dungarth.'

'Ah, I see, go on.'

'Well the Earl had overrun the island and did not wish the queen to hold out, merely to surrender without further bloodshed, so he cut off the landward side and summoned her to give up. The story goes that she appeared on the rampart and taunted him and he was further inflamed by her beauty and courage. He gave her until dawn the following day to change her mind and when she had not done so he attacked. His men overran the dun without opposition and when they got inside a great flock of ravens rose from the ground. But there were no warriors, no Queen, nothing.'

'And the Queen, what happened to her?'

Sonia shrugged. 'History won't tell. Legend says she will return one day, bringing a new race of rulers to the island.'

'And d'you think that's likely ... I mean that the queen will return?'

'It's possible, in this island you can believe anything like that might happen; the islanders still call an easterly wind an invader's wind, yet few of them know why. I thought you might be the Queen, for you were somehow, I don't know, the way I have always imagined the Queen might have been, a real woman ... Oh you mustn't laugh at me! If I'd known you would laugh I would never have told you!' Sonia was furious but Justine reached out a hand and restrained her.

'My dear, I believe your story may well be true.' Seeing the look in Sonia's face Justine regretted the sudden loss of rapport with the girl. Very gently she said, 'I will tell you that here, on Ynyscraven, I feel a strange peace. You are right about my purpose here. Why should I conceal it? What happens here will make me like a queen. No my dear, I was simply laughing at myself and the irony if I, at my age, were to conceive a child, never mind a race of kings.'

Sonia breathed a sigh of relief, then had another idea. 'Have you a daughter then, of child-bearing age?'

This time the smile disappeared entirely from Justine's face.

The two women talked a little more. Justine confided in her, surprising herself that she could, and wanted to, talk to this strange, fey creature. At last the girl rose. 'It is late,' she said. 'As you are alone I'll light you up to your room, I know the house and can find my way back. Nobody locks their doors at night so I can slip away.' Sonia picked up the lamp and led Justine into the hall.

Inside Justine's bedroom Sonia put down the lamp on the washstand. She moved the jug and ewer out of the way and put a mirror on the marble. Then she pulled up a chair. 'There you are,' she said, indicating the chair.

Justine sat down and picked up her hair

brush. She was about to say goodnight when the girl took the brush gently from her hand and began to brush Justine's black tresses in long sensuous sweeps. For a minute Justine was embarrassed, then she closed her eyes. It had been a long day and the sensation was delicious. She thought of her bedroom in Porth Ardur and the lonely ministrations she had submitted herself to.

For several minutes neither said anything. Then Sonia spoke. 'My father, who ruined my mother by seducing her, was a Slav count. Sometimes my mother calls me her 'petite vicomtesse.' I suppose it is alright for a vicomtesse to dress the hair of a queen.'

'I have no objection,' answered Justine in that low, sensual voice that she could not help using at such times.

Sonia saw the scarlet ribbon lying on the bed and caught up the hair in a thick tail behind Justine's head. She gently patted it. 'There, the raven's wings are folded ...'

Slowly Justine rose from the chair and her skirt slipped to the floor. She peeled her blouse back from her shoulders. 'Good night, my dear,' she said, gently dismissing Sonia.

'Good night,' whispered the girl.

the Captain.

Charlie
behind them. T

Different Ships, Different Longsplices

Caryatid anchored off Ynyscraven Lighthouse on Monday evening. Charlie oper-
ated the semaphore arms and Captain
Macready, together with his Chief Mate
Foster, went ashore. They were met at
the landing by the keepers and Macready
and Foster briefed the latter on the job the
ship's crew intended doing. An hour later
Caryatid steamed into the anchorage at the
southern end of Ynyscraven and brought
up to her anchor. The final preparations
for the rigging of the new hoist wire having
been made, Captain Macready gave his
ship's company a watch ashore.

At the gangway door Foster watched
the last grinning fireman into the boat
and waved the coxswain away. 'Back at
midnight, lads,' he called after them as
with a roar of its engine the boat turned
away from *Caryatid*'s side.

Foster met the boat when it returned and Captain Macready came down to leave the ship. 'Farthing coming?' asked the Captain.

'Here sir,' puffed Charlie, hurrying along.

'Er, Bernard,' began Macready rather bashfully, 'I've been invited to stay ashore, send a boat in at eight o'clock, will you?'

'Yes, of course, sir. Where will you be, at the reeve's house?'

Macready had not the foggiest idea where he would be except that it would be in the arms of Justine. He nearly forgot himself and answered facetiously. In the end he guessed. 'Yes, yes that's right ... ah, here comes the boat.'

'Back at midnight, Charlie,' said Foster to the second mate.

Charlie just grinned. He had four hours before midnight.

'She's in, she's in!' Justine looked up from her book. Sonia was running across the grass towards the house, her hair loose behind her. 'The *Caryatid*'s just anchored,' she explained, bursting breathlessly in. Justine rose, her heart thumping like a hammer. Sonia's eyes were shining like sunstruck spray. 'Come *on!*' She led the way into the hall.

'Where are we going?' asked Justine bemusedly, following Sonia up the stairs.

She followed the girl into the main bedroom. From the window the view commanded the last ten yards of the path from the landing before it forked.

'We wait here until the crew have gone past. Then the officers will come up.'

'So you're waiting for one of the officers?'

'Yes!' answered Sonia, standing beside the window, concealed from outside by the curtain. Justine frowned, suddenly moral. 'You're *not* having an affair with Bernard Foster, are you?' she asked incredulously.

'Who's Bernard Foster? No, Charlie is *my* darling!' They both laughed. The garden was already in shadow. Night rolled up from the east in a cloudless sky. A gaggle of heads appeared; untidily, noisily and thirstily *Caryatid*'s crew filed up the path beside the reeve's house treading a path once used by Celtic monks.

'Oh, we don't consider *them* invaders,' explained Sonia, uncannily reading Justine's mind. 'They're rather sweet really. There's one old chap that's madly in love with my mother. He's a fireman, they are old friends, it's really quite touching.'

'What, that old people should like each other's company?'

'No, that they should get on so well. I don't expect he'd want to know her if he knew she was the daughter of an Earl.'

'So you are ...?'

'The bastard of a philandering Slav count and begot upon the body of—'

'No, no I didn't mean—'

'You meant to ask if I was related to an Earl. Well, Mother was the last Earl's sister. When she became pregnant by a Slave emigré she was disowned by her family, I don't know why, for the males made a profession of getting bastards off anybody who would oblige. The old Earl died when I was about three and his son, my cousin, took pity on us. He gave us the cottage on Ynyscraven. Here they come.'

The figures of the Captain and Charlie approached the crest of the path.

The two women went downstairs and out across the lawn. There the men saw them. It struck Macready then that this was neither the time nor the place for further dissembling and that the next few days could not be concealed from the world, at least the tiny world of Ynyscraven, without blighting the pleasure of them.

'My dear ... ' he said, striding through the wicket gate with extended arms.

Justine drew him inside the house.

On the grass Charlie and Sonia buried their tongues in each other's mouths and ground their impatient bodies together. Charlie had scarcely noticed the Captain's disappearance or with whom he had disappeared.

After a little Sonia pulled away. 'Before we go any further, and,' she flashed him a smile of pleasure at his presence, 'before Mother disappears to the Craven Arms, we had better go and introduce you to her.'

They walked across the turf and out

through the gate, leaving the house silent behind them.

'Before we get there, Charlie, I need to tell you something of my mother ...' Sonia told him her mother's sad history. 'Please don't take too much notice if she's a little odd,' she concluded.

Inside the reeve's house Captain Macready was slowly being enchanted. The idea of spending this idyll in a house of their own far exceeded his wildest imaginings. It was as though some sympathetic angel watched over their forbidden love, nurturing it tenderly even down to the details. That Faith was simple and accepted the Captain's presence without demur only served to heighten the lovers' intense awareness of each separate moment they were together. They did not hasten to bed as young people might have done, they savoured their intimacy, pretending it was a normal life they were leading, guessing they might have to live on the memory of these stolen days for a long, long time.

When at last their bodies melted together

they found that each had fulfilled its promise for the other and their hopes and imaginings had not been in vain.

Sonia and her mother lived in a stone cottage on the southern extremity of Ynyscraven. Ducking under the low doorway, Charlie found himself in a long room with a fireplace in the centre of the rear wall. There were no windows in any side other than the south wall through which they had entered. One other door, of recent creation, had been knocked in the east wall and gave onto a sort of lean-to conservatory. A few pots and pans were hung over the fireplace, which was occupied by a wood-burning range and an overmantel burdened down by artefacts, objects and beachcombed rubbish. Remaining wall space was filled with weirdly executed paintings and crude shelves of books, many of which were quite ancient, their leather bindings clearly suffering from the effects of Ynyscraven's damp. Furniture was sparse. At each end was a bed and washstand with a goatskin rug indicating a minimal concession to comfort. In the centre, occupying the greater part of the cottage, ran an enormously long refectory table which had a number of ill assorted chairs tucked under it, groaning under a burden of clothing, bits of wood and miscellania. Unwashed crockery littered the table, along with some sheets of paper bearing indecipherable scribbles.

'Mother's an artist ...' explained Sonia, as she led the wondering Charlie through into the conservatory.

'Hullo, Mother,' she said. 'This is Charlie. We're very fond of each other.'

Charlie had seen her before without really absorbing details. She was working on a panel less odd than the work in the main room. She turned and stared at him.

Sonia's mother was in fact not yet fifty. She had a thin, weathered, striated appearance, like sea-eroded iron in which the weaker metal has oxidised and left a grain-like pattern of tough, durable material that gave the impression of greater

242

age. Her face was oval and drawn, her mouth no more than a pale gash beneath a nose that clearly indicated a fondness for drink. Her hair was lank and straight. She was at once old and not so old. Feeble and strangely strong.

'Fond?' she asked in a voice that was surprisingly and undeniably refined. 'Fond?' she repeated rising to survey Charlie. She wore about her neck a skein of dull stones and beads that looked like sea-tumbled pebbles. Her dress was a once-fashionable black crépe garment that hung about her like a black shift. Beneath it she apparently wore little else for the thin material lifted over the points of her breasts, a fact of which Calico Jack had not been unaware. They were oddly incongruous compared to her slim hips and the thinness of her wrists and ankles.

'So she's fond of you, eh?'

'And I of her, ma'am,' began Charlie.

'And you'll be wanting to seduce her, I'll warrant; you young men are all the same.'

'Mother!'

'You be quiet, my dear. I'll trouble you to hold your tongue until I've finished with this fellow.' She wagged a paintbrush under Charlie's nose until he had to move his face back to avoid having his nostrils painfully penetrated.

'Now you listen to me. I'm not having you mess about with my daughter unless you're decent. My family's been a victim to whoredom and whore-masters for generations; Sonia's different. She's an island bird that'll never leave Ynyscraven. There are spirits of ruined, raped women all over this rock, hundreds of 'em. Widows, mothers, sisters, wives. All the dead come here to keen over men lost on the rocks in shipwrecks, in rapine and bloody murder ...' There was quite a lot more, but Charlie could not make head or tail of it and eventually stopped listening. Instead he looked politely at the panel on which the old woman had been working. He recognised it at once as an inn sign for the Craven Arms.

Eventually the old woman fell silent.

'They are the Craven Arms, are they?'

asked Charlie changing the subject.

The woman looked at the panel. 'Yes,' she said slowly. 'Three ravens sable upon a ground blanc ... the 'C' is a phonetic addition to the island's name. It is added to the word to make it easier for persons unused to the true tongue to cope with. Sonia, light the lamps inside and tell the young man the history of the island.' Sonia smiled at Charlie and returned into the cottage. Charlie was about to follow but the woman detained him. 'Young man, do you love my daughter?'

Charlie looked down at her. It was growing dark and alone in the glass room he felt oddly frightened, as if she possessed some power that drew strength from her feebleness compared with his youthful vigour; as though her knowledge and experience outweighed all his physical advantages. Her eyes held his and he saw now where Sonia inherited her green irises. Yet Sonia's lacked the fire that burned fever-bright within her mother's. Charlie was suddenly afraid of the tremendous power in this woman's brain that blazed out through her eyes, a power of knowledge that grasped portents and formed oracles.

Was it thus that Cassandra entered the house of Agamemnon?

'Do you love her?' the woman hissed at him, the urgency of her question slicing through the air between them so that the reflex answer that he hastily uttered was true.

'Yes!'

The woman shot out a hand and touched his face. The fingers were dry yet sensitive. Charlie was later to see her touch pebbles and sea-smoothed driftwood in this way, as if learning their nature and shape, like a blind person.

At last she seemed satisfied.

'Then you shall have her.'

There was a pause. Charlie was shaking, so tense was the atmosphere. 'Young man, beware the invader's wind, for I smell it coming and with it the scent of death ... now go into the house and Sonia will tell you the history of Ynyscraven and of the ravens of Dungarth.'

'Mother likes you,' said Sonia, leaning her head on Charlie's shoulder. The two of them were slowly descending the path to the landing. Above and behind them they could hear the approach of *Caryatid*'s watch ashore, a drunken, joyous riot that spilled out of the dark night and down the cliff like a freshet.

Charlie felt the yielding waist and turned her, crushing her suppleness to the hardening urgency of his own body. Around them the rocky crannies of Ynyscraven gave off the sweet scent of growing ferns.

Back in his bunk aboard *Caryatid*, Charlie pondered on the events of the evening. Coming down the path Sonia had told him the rest of her mother's history. There was little in her appearance or her behaviour to give the slightest clue as to her blue blood. Perhaps that was explained away by her madness or her eccentricity. No, there was more to the older woman than the eccentricity produced by aristocratic genetics. Had Charlie glimpsed a soul in some kind of torment within the crackling fire of those green eyes? Then another thought struck him. A disquieting, sinister thought that reeked of the old, cynical, pre-Porth Ardur Charlie. Was this old woman the obverse of the romantic coin of the island? Was she the toad under the stone? Or a witch?

Charlie inevitably thought of Sonia, steeped as she was in the history of this granite and shale heap of inhospitable rock. Was she touched with the same poison? Was it poison, isolation or the island that had turned the old woman's mind, or perhaps the other suffering?

Charlie did not even know the nature of the old woman's madness except that when he had pressed Sonia, she had shrugged and fallen silent. He drifted into sleep regretting that one could obtain a First Mate's Certificate without the slightest knowledge of psychology.

Sonia returned to the cottage. Her mother was still about, decanting gorse wine from a jug. She poured a beaker, for her daughter and regarded the girl.

'You could do worse, *ma petite vicomtesse*,' she said at last. 'He does not have the look of a libertine.' Sonia said nothing, used to her mother's moods and knowing when to keep silent.

'I suppose you must have a man?' Sonia held her tongue. She lowered her eyes in a tiny, affirmative gesture, blushing and betraying herself more than at any time up on the spine of Ynyscraven.

The old woman rocked on her chair. 'Yes,' she hissed at last, 'that is our tragedy ... we must have our men.'

She took a deep draught of the wine and staggered to her feet. Sonia helped her gently to the bed. She felt her mother's shoulders heaving with sobs.

Not mad, Sonia thought, just smashed to pieces.

Captain Macready woke the following morning to the sight of sunlight flooding horizontally into the bedroom and the sound of birdsong.

He remembered the night and looked

at Justine. She lay on her back, one arm upflung behind her head. Around her face cascaded her black hair, one lock of which had fallen across her cheek, giving her a youthfully carefree appearance. Sleep was kind to her, smoothing the lines upon her face so that her lashes lay like a young bride's, trembling slightly with the dreams behind them.

Septimus smiled a smile of adoration. There was no cheap male triumph in his face. He wore the look of an angel, albeit a damned angel.

He knew he would not sleep again and rose carefully from the bed, shivering slightly as his feet touched the polished boards of the floor. He padded over to the window splendidly aware of his own nakedness, scratching the hair mat over his chest. At the window the sun hit him, not three degrees above the horizon, well north of east at this season, blazing its burning welcome to a magnificent day. Macready shut his eyes, drew a deep breath in through his nostrils and stretched the sleep out of his middle-aged body.

Then he slid up the sash window and looked out.

'God bless my soul!'

On the lawn below him a naked woman was bent over picking mushrooms. At the squeal of the window she had stopped, though remaining doubled up. Her flanks and legs were thin, lank hair hung from her shoulders and pendulous breasts sagged towards the ground. Macready felt breath on his shoulder.

'What is it?' Justine, heavy with sleep stood beside him. She too was naked.

The three stood looking at each other. In the garden, Sonia's mother straightened up, a strange wan creature, witchlike with a basket on her arm.

Instinctively Macready put his arm around Justine, pulling her closer to him so that they stood framed in the window. For a long time they stood thus, an incongruous tableau, each waiting for something to break the odd spell that seemed wound about them.

Macready felt a sudden surge of guilt, caught like this. Justine, closer to truth, felt a twinge of pity for the older woman whose identity she guessed. In the garden Sonia's mother felt her mind spin. The man and the woman were not the reeve and his wife, they were out of place, spectral and beautiful. The man's face was familiar ... she fought off a fog that seemed to threaten her sight ... they looked so happy ... one flesh ...

The old woman inclined her head and dropped into a curtsey. It was a ridiculous attitude and Septimus opened his mouth to snort at it indignantly. But Justine was too quick for him. She put her hand over his mouth.

'No, my darling, you don't understand.' Macready turned to look at her. He bent to kiss her and she slid her hand down over his belly. He began to kiss her neck, arousingly. She yielded, turning her head again to the garden. The old woman was bowing herself backwards down the garden, as if from a throne.

Justine smiled to herself and let Macready slide inside her.

Two hours later Macready stood, brass-bound and breakfasted, on the bridge of *Caryatid*. It was in truth a magnificent morning. Hardly a breath of air ruffled the surface of the sea so that the cry of the sea birds came to his ears clear and unmuted. The cliffs at the northern end of the island loomed forbidding above the ship's bow. He rang 'Stop' on the telegraph and crossed the bridge. He was manoeuvring *Caryatid* much closer in than was customary.

'Hard a starboard!' The quartermaster answered and Macready pulled the two telegraph handles back to 'Half Astern'. Below the bells jingled then answered on the bridge. *Caryatid* began to tremble. He rang the port engine to 'Stop' and watched astern as the ship turned.

When the *Caryatid* had completed her turn to her Master's satisfaction he ordered, 'Midships!'

Ringing the port engine full astern to deaden the swing he called out to Foster forward: 'Leggo!'

With a splash and a roar of veering

cable the starboard bower anchor dropped from the hawse pipe as *Caryatid* gathered sternway.

Macready watched the stern. He had to drive *Caryatid* into the gut between the main cliffs and the off-lying rocks where the heavy hoist wire was secured. He had also to keep control of her or—he did not think about what might happen. He rang 'Stop' on both engines. The marble green-white of the stern-wash died away and the hiss of its fading convolutions moved past the bridge. He waved.

The motor boat which had been sent in ahead to place seamen on two selected rocks, surged forward, closing the counter. A roar from her engine and she spun, heading ashore towing the brown snake of a coir mooring line from the starboard quarter. 'Hold on forrard!' called Macready to the Mate.

Caryatid stretched her cable and the boat came back for a line from the other quarter. Within a few minutes she was moored with her stern well into the gut. From there her deck machinery could assist replacing the heavy hoist wire.

Captain Macready leaned out of the wheelhouse window, 'Alright, Bernard. She'll do there, let's get the lads going, there's a lot to do.'

There certainly was a great deal to do. Charlie soon found that Bernard had not been exaggerating when he said the work was gruelling. Although a simple operation in theory, the practical problems involved seemed legion. The distances, heights, weights and power requirements seemed to dwarf the *Caryatid*'s limited resources of machinery and manpower. It reminded Charlie of one of those lectures at the Board of Trade, where marvels are done on a blackboard and every sailor worth his salt knows the practical hitches involved render the whole exercise futile. What he had not realised that here, in this forgotten, taken-for-granted little service, such problems were met head-on and overcome.

Charlie's admiration for Bernard Foster increased enormously. The Mate seemed to be everywhere. Skidding down the hoist wire in a box loosening shackles, easing back on the great tackles that took the wire's tension from its securing screws prior to letting it go, scrambling over rocks checking on the grouting in the eyes that secured the end of the wire ... the list of the Mate's activities seemed endless. Charlie did what he could, chiefly from the boats, but he was certainly a tired man as on each successive evening he trooped ashore behind the *Caryatid*'s crew as they made for the path leading upwards to the Craven Arms.

The routine was soon established and pints of gleaming beer were already set up on the bar when, on the second evening of her stay at Ynyscraven, *Caryatid*'s crew burst like a discharge of grape-shot into the open hall of the pub.

The majority of the greasers, firemen and seamen rolled ashore to roister and drink. And drink they did, threatening to deplete the Arms' supply before the *Plover* was due to replenish it. They sang, danced and yarned, they boasted and argued and at the end of each evening they staggered, slithered or were dragged down the shaly path to the landing. Each morning the boat came in for the Captain and, minutes later, *Caryatid* weighed from the anchorage and steamed the couple of miles to the lighthouse where her men, fighting off hangovers, sweated the beer out of themselves until the steamer again moved south for her night anchorage and another watch ashore.

Without doubt it was not the exhausted seamen who presided over the drunken revels. The elderly fireman Calico Jack seemed to have taken on a new lease of energy since the ship began working at Ynyscraven. The old madwoman who kept him company was usually already in the Arms when the crew arrived and in that self-mocking, amusing way seamen have, the crowd seemed to gather round the old couple as though they formed a court.

The old woman always wore her fur coat but, despite the efforts of *Caryatid*'s less gentlemanly crew members, none found out whether or not she was naked beneath it. She hardly spoke and the men soon took her presence for granted.

One night, tired with effort and too much drink the conversation began to plumb the depths of philosophy in an illinformed, maudlin way.

Asked for his opinion Calico Jack, who was nodding gently to himself, threw up his head and called defiantly: 'Love! Love is what makes the world go round!'

There were cheers. 'That's bleedin' original,' said someone. But Jack was not to be gainsaid.

'Love will make a man do mad things!' There was a chorus of assent from the crowd. Most were thinking of some riotous night in Santos, Sydney or Yokohama where the sense their mothers had given them succumbed to their fathers' legacy of lust.

'I mind a bosun once,' began Jack and there were shushes of silence around the table. 'I mind a bosun once who staked all on love and was ruined by it.'

'How was that then, Calico?'

'Shut yer face an' you'll find out, won't

yer,' added a shipmate helpfully.

'I was on a fleet oiler once, would you believe we burned coal in our own boiled bloody daft Admiralty.' Jack quaffed his pint and drained it.

'Buy 'im another, look you ...'

Calico Jack sipped from his refilled glass. 'This bosun you see, 'e fell in love with a young seaman who was, it has to be admitted, a fine-lookin' fellow. All the officers called him Billy Budd after some book or other. Well, you see, this bosun was very unpopular because he shopped an old queen of a fireman what'd made passes at this young lad and the fireman, who was harmless anyway, got into trouble. Anyway, none of the crew liked the bosun because the loss of the fireman meant no one got drinks bought for them anymore.' Calico Jack swallowed a mouthful of beer.

'One day this seaman, Billy Budd, comes into the messroom with a letter. Says, "What'll I do about this, boys?" an' shows us like. Well, the letter was one of them love letters, fairly dripping with passion, see. We all has a laugh, see, then notices the seaman's cut up about it. Well 'e would be, wouldn't he? I mean the bosun's the bosun and can make life pretty bad for a fellow.

'Anyway the letter said that if this lad liked the bosun, would he hang his towel out through his port-hole the next morning.'

An appreciative ripple ran through the *Caryatid*'s crew. Even those who had heard the story before, or those who guessed at the ending, leaned forward eagerly.

'Next mornin' all the crowd are having tea on deck when along comes the bosun. Young Billy sidles up to him and gives him his mug of tea, but don't say a word, see. Bosun takes his tea and walks kind of slowly over to the rail. Puts his foot on lower rail, casual like and leans his elbows on the cappin'. Everybody's watching, see. Bosun looks over the rail, very casual like. Sees fifty-seven towels all hanging out of portholes ...' Laughter exploded round the room. The barman joined in the guffaws and screeches of delight at

Calico Jack's story.

Eventually it died away.

'But it ruined the bosun, see. Eight years he'd been on that ship, an' a good bosun ... drunk too much after that and went over the side not six months later. Terribly destructive thing, love ...'

The old woman beside Calico Jack reached out a hand and gripped his arm. The two smiled at each other. 'All right, mother?' said Calico Jack solicitously.

Every night Macready and Charlie walked up the hill together. 'Mr Foster's doing all the watches,' explained Charlie on the third night as they paced slowly up the hill.

'Good man, Mr Foster, good man.'

'Yes, indeed, sir.'

They walked on, the cool evening damp of the island settling round them like a cloak. Macready writhed internally. In a few minutes they would reach the wicket gate where Justine and Sonia were usually chatting. The women seemed to get on so well while their two lovers, rank-bound and stilted, came up together yet worlds apart. In the end Macready decided to chance the young man's scorn.

'I'm a married man, Mr Farthing. I'm trusting your discretion not to mention these dinners I'm having with-er-h'm Mrs ...' He mumbled the name which came as a poor contrast to the emphasis he had laid on 'dinners'. Charlie smiled to himself. Bloody long dinners that lasted until eight the next morning. They could see the two women now.

'Not a word, Captain Macready. She's a fine-looking woman.'

Macready basked in the young man's approval, but was wise enough to hold his tongue from further chatter.

Every evening Justine had a simple meal prepared for the Captain. It was his task to clear it away while she slipped out and prepared for their night of bliss. When she was ready she called him in that low mellifluous voice of hers, so that his name echoed through the dark, still house.

The bedroom was always perfumed with fresh flowers new cut from the reeve's garden, the curtains always drawn and a low-burning oil lamp always threw the room into sensuous chiaroscuro.

Charlie and Sonia did not experience the sense of urgency and desperation that influenced Justine and the Captain. They suffered the pangs of youth. Eagerness and inexperience in such circumstances are often our first introduction to the dichotomous nature of life. The ambivalence of the situation seems to demand a decision by each or both of the parties. Made together in favour of succumbing to the natural urges the couple can experience the joys of coitus, and, unprepared, risk the consequences. Made independently either rape ensues or deep wounds are left on one or other. However, a degree of maidenly modesty veiling healthy curiosity is usually enough to curb outright male lust and encourage it to follow less consequential activities.

Not that Charlie was totally without experience with women. But the mechanics of distant couplings seemed very remote from this turmoil he was experiencing in his manly bosom with Sonia. She coyly assuaged his more urgent needs and he knew the scent and feel of her breasts, withholding a final violation of her deepest intimacy only because she promised him heaven at a later date.

In the meantime they walked and talked, watching the last embers of each succeeding day flare out their last to the west-north-west of the island.

'Tomorrow Charlie, I promise you ... everything.'

'Why not tonight, Sonia? I love you ... I never want to leave you ... you've nothing to fear ... I promise ... Sonia, I *want* to marry you.' She silenced him with a kiss and dragged him down into the damp heather.

Charlie lay on his back and Sonia lay on his chest. Her breath was warm on his face. 'It's special for a girl, Charlie, the first time. I just want it all to be right.' She kissed him again. He reached for her breasts.

'No, Charlie, lie down.' She pushed him

firmly back, then in a swift movement moved her hand to his belt. For a minute Charlie was too annoyed with the rebuff to react. When he did so it was too late.

He felt her cool hand extract his latent member. It burned to a rigidity that took her breath away. 'Tomorrow,' she whispered to him later as he lay gasping on the ground.

Charlie worked at the lighthouse the following day in high good humour. He stripped to the waist in the boats, bronzing himself in Sonia's honour. The new wire was hoisted and stretched. Foster was down reshackling the new securing eyes for the ancilliary wires onto the heavy main one. The sun burned and again there was no wind.

In the reeve's house Justine had finished lunch and had selected a book from the library to read on the lawn when she heard a voice in the hall.

'Who is it?' she called.

'Me. Sonia.'

'Come in, then.' The girl was hesitant,

standing diffidently by the door.

'Thank you, it's a beautiful day, isn't it?'

Justine smiled, recollecting the girl had said something about being able to ask her anything.

'It is, my dear, but that wasn't what you came here to ask, was it?'

'No. Is the maid about?'

'She's washing up, come into the library, we won't be disturbed.'

'Justine?'

Justine turned, caught in the act of opening the door. 'Yes?'

'You won't laugh about what I've come to ask?'

'Of course not. Come on in.'

The two women passed into the library and the door closed.

Justine took Macready's arm as usual when the Captain reached the wicket gate. They walked slowly over the lawn towards the house. Justine watched Sonia lead Charlie up the side path towards the pub.

'Not many more evenings like this,

my dear,' said Macready gloomily, then receiving no reply asked, 'What is it?'

Justine was waving to Sonia who looked over her shoulder and waved back.

'Sonia.'

'What about Sonia? What's she carrying that bunch of campion for?'

'She's going to her wedding, Septimus.'

'I don't understand ...'

'It doesn't matter, love, come inside.'

Sonia led Charlie up through the old monastery gate and on to the high path. They strode purposefully past the pub and the cluster of dwellings that constituted Main Street. Charlie's questions were silenced and it was all he could do, after his day's work, to keep up with his guide. On their left a magnificent sunset was building up, gilding high cirrus clouds so that they looked like golden horse tails flickering across the sky.

After half an hour's relentless walk, when Charlie was very close to losing his equanimity, Sonia slowed her pace and dropped back alongside him.

She took his hand. 'Remember what I told you about the Ravens of Dungarth, Charlie?'

'Yes, of course.'

Sonia pointed. Ahead of him Charlie could see a low ridge set hard-edged against the flaming sky. There was something commandingly artificial about the ridge. It curved away towards the edge of the cliff.

'Is this the place?'

'Yes,' she whispered. 'This is Dun-Garth. Come on.'

They walked slowly now up the glacis, over ground that the Norman Earl and his war-band must have passed over nine centuries earlier, to breast the final ridge.

Before them in an irregular circle ran the remains of the rampart. Apart from the isthmus upon which they had approached, the cliffs fell away sheer to the Atlantic. There was no escaping from the place except by the narrow neck of land. In the centre of the bare circle stood a sarsen stone. Sonia led Charlie towards it. At its base they sat down. No word passed between them as, hand in hand, they simply watched the last of the daylight bleed out of the western sky. The campion in Sonia's hand wilted.

There was hardly any wind down on the sea, but up on the cliff top there was just sufficient to set up a low moan around the tip of the sarsen stone. It mingled with the moans of the two lovers at its foot.

Just before midnight, Calico Jack decided to overstay his leave. He had tottered into the hutch that, equipped with a stone trough, served the Craven Arms for a urinal and spewed the contents of his stomach up. He felt his head clear and moved to re-enter the pub when the old woman approached him. She had followed him from the bar, and now stood in his way. There was light enough for him to see her as she slowly opened her fur coat. Calico Jack blinked at the barely discernible breasts and the dark triangle below them.

'Come on Jack, come to my house, I'm in need of a man.'

As a young woman Sonia's mother had succumbed to the plausible nonsense spouted by a young, very handsome Slav count. He had been in town for the season and decided to seduce the prettiest woman under his host's roof.

His victim had yielded almost from the first, but the realisation of the true nature of what most called 'love' had both repelled and fascinated her. The physical pain she experienced that first time had combined with a revulsion for the way her 'lover' had so roughly handled her to leave her with a feeling of antipathy for men. When, nine months later, she had borne Sonia, her mind had been affected, a condition that was scarcely helped by her family's reaction.

Her banishment to Ynyscraven, however, had been the saving of something of her shattered life, for here she had been able to find herself. She had taken up painting, wild-tortured work at one with the landscape she found herself in. She had steeped herself and her daughter in the island and everything about it, earning a precarious living and receiving a small allowance from the present Earl.

But though disliking the sex, she still occasionally sought out the company of men. It was difficult to discern the precise nature of her obsession unless it was to return to her youth, to try again and discover if love, as she had been conditioned to think of it, was possible, or whether it was all a terrible, terrible deception. She had dreaded the time when Sonia would come to her and say she was leaving with a young man. And now it had happened.

He had seemed a pleasant young man, without the blandishments of her Slav count and the thought of her daughter being truly loved ... she shook off the image but it returned to haunt her. What had she missed, what had she missed?

Calico Jack walked beside her, stumbling on the uneven path. He banged his head on the lintel as she led him inside her cottage and lit a lamp.

Jack leaned against the door and blinked.

His experienced eye located the bed. The old woman turned and slid the fur coat onto the floor. Matter-of-factly Calico Jack peeled the cotton cap from his head and the shirt from his torso. The remnants of a fine physique appeared. The old woman watched as his spindle shanks stepped out of the dungaree trousers.

Victor of many a brothel sortie, drunk or sober, Calico Jack did not fail now. His was not the clumsy eagerness of Charlie, nor the yet sprightly love of Septimus, his was the tired desire of one human's company for another. Perhaps Calico Jack was the greatest lover of the three, for when he drifted into sleep the old woman cradled his bald head on her shoulder, crooned endearments into his unhearing ear and dreamed of glittering ballrooms and the bustles that women wore a million years ago.

Charlie and Sonia lay till a midnight chill drove them from Dun-Garth. Ambling contentedly south, wordless and wondering, they came to the ruins of the old

Celtic monastery. Beneath an arch and remnant of roof they made love again before falling asleep.

Hours later a wraith of fog licked them from their hole and, running and jumping to restore circulation, they burst into the cottage in search of a hot drink.

Sonia's mother was not there.

'Gathering mushrooms, I expect,' explained Sonia, brushing her hair from her mouth and smiling happily at Charlie who never took his eyes from her. She handed him a steaming mug and came round the table to sit on his lap.

Captain Macready rose from the bed, aware that the fog was present before he reached the window. He threw up the window and sniffed the air.

'Not too bad,' he muttered. 'It'll clear by nine or so, must be able to see about—Good God!'

'What is it, Septimus?' called Justine languidly from the bed.

'I'm not sure.'

Macready could see the lawn below.

though the hedge and wicket gate were lost to view in the white mist. Out of the fog, bent over, were two apparitions. Calico Jack and Sonia's mother picked mushrooms like two superannuated water babies, naked and grotesque, yet oddly appropriate on this strange island.

'They're rock sprites,' said Justine beside him, the sheet drawn about her against the damp chill. There was bubbling laughter in her voice. 'If you watch them they'll fade into the background.'

The male goblin straightened, looking up and saw the two lovers in the window.

'Mornin', Captain,' said Calico Jack, cool as the fog, as if he was meeting Macready on the quay at Porth Ardur. The woman looked up, then she moved, almost swiftly, to stand beside the man. The two couples stood looking at each other for a few seconds then Calico Jack winked and resumed picking mushrooms, moving away into the fog. The old woman lingered a moment then smiled. She too moved off into the fog. But she did not retreat.

Charlie was about to leave the cottage when Sonia's mother returned with Calico Jack. He retired into the house astonished at the two basket-bearing figures that shambled unconcernedly into the parlour. Sonia flickered him a warning glance and equally insouciantly made more tea.

'Good morning, Mr Farthing,' said Calico, stepping into his dungarees and accepting the mug from Sonia. Still naked the old woman cracked four herring gull eggs into a bowl and began to whip an omelette into which she dropped the chopped mushrooms.

Charlie and Calico Jack started down to the boat with a breakfast inside them. 'I remember a time in BA when a mate and myself knocked off a mother and her daughter. *They* made us breakfast as well ...'

Calico broke the spell for Charlie. He suddenly remembered he had overstayed his leave.

They met Captain Macready at the wicket gate. Justine was kissing him goodbye. She was wrapped in a peignoir.

'Morning, Captain,' repeated Calico, winking again, conspiratorily.

'Morning, Evans, and you too, Mr Farthing ... goodbye, my dear—' Red-faced, Macready tore himself out of Justine's arms. Behind him he could hear her low chuckle. The three men strode down the path in silence. The fog thickened as they descended to the beach. In the white silence they could hear men's voices, then the chug of the motor boat's engine. Macready stopped. Out of deference the other two stopped as well.

'I'm displeased by your behaviour, both of you, particularly yours, Mr Farthing, you should know better as an officer. Evans I'd expect it of, but not you.'

Charlie hung his head in genuine embarrassment. He felt terrible, respecting old Macready as he did. He burned with shame at the thought of what he and Sonia had been doing, as if this dressing down made it all cheap and like some one-night stand with a whore in, where was it? Buenos Aires?

276

'As, however, we are all gentlemen of the world this matter will go no further unless Mr Foster brings you up, Mr Farthing, or the Chief brings you up, Evans, in which case I shall have no alternative but to do something. D'you understand?' They both mumbled their thanks. The boat engine was loud now. Then it shut off and there was the scrunch of bows on shingle and the shout of the bowman leaping ashore.

'Now, gentlemen, you go on ahead and pretend to hide under the canopy. I'll follow. One word of any of this and—' Macready left the threat hanging in mid air. He was himself aware that he was on very thin ice. Relieved, Calico Jack and Charlie turned gratefully away, loping downwards with the air of schoolboys out of bounds.

Breaking Strain

Charlie did not get away with his night adrift. Calico Jack did. He stood so many watches for firemen living in Porth Ardur that no one really questioned his absence. For Charlie it was different.

Caryatid did not move from the anchorage until about noon when the fog finally lifted. During the forenoon Bernard Foster came quietly into Charlie's room and sat himself down. Charlie was dozing on his bunk. Foster lit his pipe and put both his feet up on the settee.

'Charlie, I'm rather disappointed in you.' He puffed and then lit another match.

Charlie sat up, flushing.

'Sorry?'

Foster looked up at him through a dense cloud of tobacco smoke. 'I know you're over the moon with this girl, but Charlie, I don't expect the Second Mate to come back with a screw-loose fireman after a night on the loose.'

Charlie swung his legs over the bunk.

'Look, Bernard, I'm sorry I overstayed my leave. It won't happen again and I realise I'm totally in the wrong, but before we go any further I've not been having a bag-off with a whore. Sonia and I intend to get married. Didn't you go a bit off the rails when you were courting Anthea?'

Foster was silent, laying a smokescreen between himself and the aggressively defensive Charlie. Had he? To tell the truth he couldn't remember. He got up, fanning the smoke away. 'Alright, Charlie, drop it, but don't do it again.' He paused, waiting for some reaction. 'And just to rub it in *I'm* going ashore tonight. It's your watch aboard.'

Charlie flopped back on his bunk. Christ! He'd really asked for that!

That evening Foster came into Charlie's cabin and threw him the store-room keys. 'The old man's gone in, I'll take the dinghy.' Foster left. Charlie felt like hell about the whole world.

Half an hour later he was aware of a familiar voice calling his name. He raced on deck and peered over the side. There, sitting in the rowing dinghy that they had been using at the lighthouse, sat Sonia. She spun the boat and brought it alongside. Making fast the line Charlie threw down, she was soon standing beside him.

'That Mr Foster met me on the path, said I'd find a boat and could get out to see you if I liked. Here I am. Oh! He said something about he'd done some remembering but that didn't make it right ... and you'd still got to do your watch. No, he said "bloody watch", that's right.' She smiled. He took her hand and led her along the alley-way.

Then he locked his cabin door.

The following evening *Sea Dragon* anchored in company with the *Caryatid*. The fog had not returned and as the shadow of the island fell over the anchorage it became the warmest, stillest night of all. Aboard *Caryatid* the grumbling watch regarded the *Sea Dragon* with ill-concealed distaste.

'Bleedin' gin palace.'

'Jus' a floating brothel.'

'It's the rich that gets the pleasure ...'

Sir Hector Blackadder had decided to have a formal dinner. He liked to alternate a formal dinner with a buffet but the anchorage was beautiful and Stanier had suggested the occasion. That Stanier wished to show off to *Caryatid*'s Master, never entered Sir Hector's mind; that Captain Macready was enjoying the flesh of Tegwyn's mother never entered Stanier's.

Dressed in his mess kit, feeling every inch the sailor, Stanier knocked discreetly on Miss Caroline's stateroom door.

'Who is it?'

'Jimmy,' he winced at the name.

'Come in.'

She was dressed in black, plainly, almost severely. Her bobbed hair and voguish looks combined with her slender figure to give her a boyish appearance. She was a stick compared to Tegwyn, and yet ... Stanier felt slightly uncomfortable as she watched him, resenting the fact that he was not quite in control of the situation and yet enjoying it.

'Well?'

'I wondered if you had an answer for me?' he asked.

She came nearer and he was suddenly aware of the way she moved. Willowy she might be, but there was a compelling power, a confident sensuality about her that he found overpowering.

She stopped just in front of him. Stanier was aware that her hard breasts barely lifted the material of her dress but she leaned backwards on her thighs, gently pushing her pelvis forward against his. She smiled into his face.

'Your answer is ready, but I'm not ready to give it. Go and have your Celtic tart for a bit longer ...' She trailed off, poking his pelvis twice more and then turning and wiggling her backside at him in an unbelievably provocative dismissal.

Stanier sat between Tegwyn and Miss Loring. Opposite was Caroline, who seemed to be watching him with a sardonic smile on her face the entire evening. She certainly discomfited poor Tegwyn, opposite whom sat Pomeroy. Samantha and Sir Hector sat facing each other while Argyle regarded Miss Loring on Caroline's right.

The saloon was warm and the cool gaze of Caroline sent Stanier's blood pressure sky high. He tried making conversation but somehow the heat seemed to enervate the whole company. Nevertheless the food was excellent and it kept the group occupied. Sweat stood out on Stanier's brow and his collar felt suffocatingly tight. He could stand it no longer and reached into the mess jacket pocket for a handkerchief.

He pulled out Justine's panties.

A cascade of brief lace dangled from his wrist as he passed it over his brow. It was only as its scent of lavender wafted past his nose that Stanier noticed.

Caroline's grin spread and Pomeroy gave an excited sort of whimper. At these two spontaneous changes of expression directed to her left, Tegwyn turned to look at Stanier. Her mouth dropped open at the same instant that Stanier realised what he was doing. He hurriedly dropped his hand and attempted to crush the garment back into his pocket.

Tegwyn was too quick for him. She snatched the panties from his hand and, with cast down eyes spread them on her lap. She recognised them instantly. Her mother bought them from a Bond Street representative who called once a year and sold her a few very exclusive items for certain ladies of Porth Ardur.

If Caroline was expecting a gaffe from Tegwyn she was disappointed. A girl who can lose her footing in a quickstep and recover it without tripping her partner can handle the discovery of her mother's panties in the pocket of her lover.

Disappointed, Caroline rose to lead the ladies out onto the quarterdeck.

In all justice to James St John Stanier it has to be admitted that on this occasion he was a victim of circumstances over which he had had very little control. However he was ready to protest his innocence and anxious to do so before Tegwyn caused a row. He therefore initiated the bedtime ritual with almost indecent haste. Tegwyn was not slow to take the hint, eager to accuse Stanier of unspeakable things. Caroline watched their flushed faces disappear. She crossed to Pomeroy who was, as far as she knew, the only other person who had really seen what happened.

'Did that amuse you, Pom?'

'A little, although I'm not sure what annoyed Tegwyn so.'

Caroline chuckled. 'It's an odd name. Coarse really.'

'But she's very beautiful,' said Pomeroy musingly.

'Pom! I'm surprised at you!'

'Oh Caro, for heaven's sake. You've been listening to that silly cat Samantha again. She thinks that anyone who doesn't fall into bed with her must be queer.'

'Have you ever been to bed with a woman, Pom?' Pomeroy was silent. 'Haven't you?'

'Once.' He said flatly. There was a bitter defeat in his voice.

'And didn't you like it?'

285

Again there was a long silence. Caroline waited expectantly.

'She didn't like me. And I had to pay her for it.'

'Poor Pom.' There was an unexpected sympathy in Caroline's voice.

Pomeroy sniffed and straightened up. 'That's enough of confessions for one night. I'm for bed.' He sounded so artificial. Caroline thought, he's really quite brave.

Pomeroy slipped into his stateroom and quickly undressed. He slipped into silk pyjamas and a silk robe. Then, lighting a cigarette he slithered across to the bulkhead and lifted down the mirror. The noise of rowdy voices from the next stateroom was dying down. He put his eye to the hole.

His heart beat faster.

He had a view of the low bunk and of Tegwyn's upper body. Her dress was off and Stanier was slavering all over her belly. He ignored the yacht's master and watched the girl's face. Her head was thrown back so that the line of her throat formed a curve as eloquent as a line by Botticelli, thought Pomeroy. Her eyes were closed but he could see the sheen of tears drying across her cheeks. Falling from her cast-back head onto the bedclothes, the blue lights dancing in its sheen, Tegwyn's hair bobbed with the quick jerking of her body.

Pomeroy did not sense the other person in his cabin until he felt breath on his neck. He whirled to face Caroline.

'Pom!' she said in mock indignation. 'You voyeur!'

Pomeroy's heart was thumping crazily. He was aware that Caroline had changed into pyjamas like himself but was non-plussed at her appearance in his cabin.

Gently she pushed him out of the way and put her eye to the hole.

He watched as her lips curved in a smile. 'Mmmmm, he's not bad. *Quelle technique* …'

Pomeroy suddenly recovered himself.

'Not him, Caro, not that fool, her!'

Caroline took her eye away and turned to look at Pomeroy. 'You mean you've been watching her?'

Pomeroy nodded unhappily. 'She's the most beautiful thing I've ever set eyes on,' he said wretchedly. 'I have collected the most exquisite *objets d'art* and never seen anything to match her.'

Caroline turned and took one more look through the hole. She began to feel indignation, jealousy even.

'Dammit, Pom, I came down here tonight to see if I could convert you.'

Pomeroy stood with his mouth hanging open. Caroline suddenly felt very foolish. 'And, by the way, don't call Captain Stanier a fool, he's going to be my husband.'

Pomeroy's jaw dropped further.

Caroline bit her lip. 'If you mention one word of that before I do, I'll let everyone know what you're up to.' She turned and left the stateroom.

Behind her, hands shaking, Pomeroy replaced the mirror.

'What d'you think of him then, Argyle?' Sir Hector lit a final cigar and poured a last large brandy.

'He seems suitable enough, Hector.' The Gael scratched his nose. 'He's determined and I'd agree fairly ruthless but he's had no business training. Although he's intelligent enough to pick a lot up I still canna understand why you didna choose someone fra' yer ain circle.'

Sir Hector shrugged. 'You must allow me a little sentiment. I've no son and I doubt that I've long to go. Ah, stop that snorting, I just met him and took an instant liking to the lad. I'd be surprised if I liked my own son as much, particularly bearing in mind his mother.'

'Och mon, yer ower hard on Ellen, she's a sick woman.'

'Sick woman or not, Ian, I'd sooner have Stanier as a son than any lad of hers.'

Argyle chuckled.

'What's amusing you?'

'I was jus' thinkin' that mebbe ye've a better son in Miss Caroline ...'

'Happen I have, my bonny friend, in which case they'll get on fine together.'

Sir Hector Blackadder rose and went to bed, happy that the matter was settled.

Argyle lingered a little longer. Then he too rose and went out onto the starlit quarterdeck.

'Samantha, Hector's away down for a wee bit o' shut-eye.'

The lissome blonde straightened up from the rail. 'Och aye, Rob Roy,' she said rudely, 'I'll away and rub his sick leg.'

From the depths of a steamer chair Miss Loring giggled. Ian Argyle looked at her. Women, he thought. Pity you couldn't set 'em off against the income tax.

An Invader's Wind

Caryatid lay at her anchor off the northern end of Ynyscraven. From her stern several fishing lines reached down into the limpid water. They were desultorily jerked to animate the feathers far below in the hope of attracting mackerel. It was the seamen's holiday, for the previous day the hoist had been completed and tested. Today the second engineer and a couple of greasers sweated up in the engine house overhauling 'all that shit and split pins', as Mackerel Jack put it.

Further forward Captain Macready sat at his desk. With a flourish he signed the report that informed the Commissioner's Secretary that the hoist wire and engine at Ynyscraven had been completely renewed and overhauled as necessary. It gave him some satisfaction, a job well done never failed to do that for the Captain, but he reflected sadly that the idyll that he and Justine had enjoyed was nearly over.

He rubbed a finger round the inside of his collar. It was hot as the hobs of hell. He ruefully thought of Justine lazing the day away in the garden. The thought was disquieting, he got up and peered out of the port hole. The gentlest of zephyrs was rippling catspaws across the blue surface of the sea.

Easterly, thought the Captain inconsequentially.

Sonia's mother sensed the coming of the wind in the preternatural stillness of the dawn. There were no mushrooms on the lawn of the reeve's house. She shuddered with more than the coolness of the air upon her bare flesh.

Sonia was up when her mother returned to the cottage. The old woman was wild-eyed and haggard.

'What's the matter, Mother?'

'The wind, Sonia. The invader's wind!'

The girl walked outside the cottage and sniffed the air. It was still as a dark pool.

She shrugged and went back inside the cottage. Later Sonia walked down to the reeve's house. Justine lay in a deck chair reading. 'Hullo, love,' she said as Sonia plumped down on the grass beside her.

'Hullo. Justine, I think they've nearly finished at the lighthouse. What'll happen to you when they sail?'

Justine smiled sadly. 'I don't know, love. I'll go back to Porth Ardur of course, carry on as normal ...' her voice trailed off.

'Will you still see the Captain?' The girl's voice was candid, open. It was a sharp contrast to the dissembling tone of Porth Ardur gossips, Justine reflected.

'Yes, we'll still dance together, I suppose.'

'Would you like to stay here on Ynyscraven, I mean forever?'

Justine laughed again, a high clear laugh. 'As a fairy tale, yes, but it is impossible. I have to live on something, I've a business to run.'

'Your daughter could do that.'

'That's true,' said Justine, a faint spark of excitement lighting in her brain. It was instantly extinguished by more practical considerations.

Aboard *Sea Dragon* the holiday party lounged, swam and drank Pimm's No. 1 cup. Samantha, long and cool, lay draped like a pair of silk stockings over a steamer chair. More compact and less comfortable, Dorothy Loring sat sweating slightly, sipping an excessive amount of Pimm's under the mistaken impression that it would quench her thirst.

Stanier had been summoned to Sir Hector's stateroom where the two men were joined by Argyle. Certain business propositions were put to Stanier. They followed the outline already sketched out for him by Caroline. Nevertheless Stanier was out of his mind with excitement at the golden road the two men laid before him. By noon the several large whiskies that Sir Hector had poured into him and the back slapping and shower of 'My boy's' that he had received from the millionaire had served to render him somewhat injudicious.

294

When the yacht's bosun reported the freshening easterly wind he dismissed the matter. It was only a force three and would die with the sun.

By afternoon it was cool enough to drive the languid Samantha from her steamer chair.

Tegwyn had woken alone and spent sometime staring at the deck-head above her. She thought over the events of the evening before and was, for the first time, ashamed of submitting to Stanier. There had been something different about him last night. He had lacked a little of that exclusive attention to herself that had so attracted her vanity at first. And the argument left a dirty taste in her mouth.

Come to think of it, he had been perceptibly cooling for some time. Tegwyn sat up, suddenly furious. She remembered several little incidents; glances; secret, covert gestures. Her rival's face blazed suddenly before her.

Caroline!

Tegwyn leapt from her bunk like a tigress. She tore the nightdress from her shoulders spitting little oaths from twisted lips. Struggling into some clothes she caught sight of herself in the mirror of the dressing table. A wild-eyed, half-hysterical Celt. God, how those stuffed shirts would laugh at her if she went out like that to row with James.

She bit her lip. Then she remembered her mother's warning. In another minute she had collapsed on the stool and her head fell forward among the powder, the hair brushes and the scent bottles.

She did not hear the gentle knocking on the door.

'May I come in?' Pomeroy entered the stateroom. He was shaking and did not trust his legs. He sat quickly on the bunk. At the sudden movement Tegwyn sat up and spun round. 'Mr Pomeroy!'

'Please do not distress yourself, Miss Tegwyn.'

'But I—'

Pomeroy could not stop himself now. He had screwed himself up to such a pitch that having come so far he felt he could not retreat.

'Miss Tegwyn, please listen to me. I want to be your friend. I know Stanier is a rogue, I've seen so many of his arrogant type at school and in business. They stop at nothing to satisfy their ambitions. They hurt anyone who is in their way.' Tegwyn had stopped crying. She was repairing the damage to her pride. She felt Pomeroy's voice caress her in an oddly soothing way. As if he understood how abused she had suddenly, revoltingly, felt.

'I've admired you from the very beginning of this cruise. I know nothing about women except that you are the most exquisite I've ever seen.' Pomeroy looked down at his carefully manicured hands. 'I love to possess beautiful things, to display them, just to touch and handle them.' There was crooning adoration in his voice now. It was utterly seductive, Tegwyn thought, as she looked at Pomeroy's tear-filled eyes. He was awaiting her derision as he must have received the scorn of many, both men and women.

'I'm a very rich man,' he whispered as though it made a difference.

Tegwyn reached out and touched his forehead.

Late in the afternoon, scending before a following sea, the *Plover* ran in to the jetty at Ynyscraven. The reeve and his wife disembarked. The *Plover* also brought a cargo of much needed beer for the Craven Arms. A real hooley was planned for *Caryatid*'s last evening.

When the engineers completed work, *Caryatid* weighed her anchor and steamed down to the southern anchorage. On her bridge Foster was remonstrating with Macready.

'I'll be frank, sir, this wind'll not die with the sun. I'm not happy about lying the night here.'

Macready said nothing. He knew that Foster was right but every nerve in his body screamed out to see Justine once more, to say his real goodbye, to mark the end of his idyll.

'You may be right, Bernard, but I don't

think it'll be too bad a blow at this time of the year. Anyway, the lads are expecting a final swan song at the Arms tonight and I don't want to disappoint them.'

'Shore leave to finish sharp at midnight then, sir?'

'Yes.'

Foster went off mumbling about standing offshore with a drunken crew. Macready felt a pang of foreboding then dismissed it. He *had* to see Justine.

Foster went down to Charlie's cabin after the ship had anchored. The Second Mate had just come off the bridge and was changing.

'Look, Charlie, I'm sorry but I want to keep you on board tonight—no, don't argue. I don't know what's got into the Old Man but he insists on giving shore leave and I'm bloody sure we'll have a gale here by midnight.'

Charlie swallowed his disappointment. Bernard had been very good to him. He owed the Mate something, even if it was only moral support.

'You'll be coming back to Ynyscraven,

Charlie, although the Old Man's acting as though he isn't.'

'Okay, Bernard.'

Up at the reeve's house Justine was welcoming the owners back. She was as charming as she could be under the circumstances but her mood revived when the reeve's wife suggested she and the Captain, as they were such good friends joined her and her husband for a sort of valedictory dinner. Of course Justine could stay longer, but if she didn't want to ... well, she was very welcome. Justine smiled her thanks. Later she went out to meet Macready a little further down the path than was usual, and out of sight of the house.

Against his better judgement Foster passed word for a watch ashore. A great gaggle of *Caryatid*'s crew struggled up the path, eyes eager for the inside of the Arms. Leading them strode Calico Jack, buoyant with the promise of a final tryst. Justine watched them pass then slipped out through the wicket gate. She saw nothing of Sonia until she had met the Captain and the pair were returning to the house, a discreet distance separating them, their voices in low and earnest conversation.

'Charlie not coming, Captain?' Sonia asked, abruptly breaking into the couple's deliberations.

'Eh?' Macready looked up. 'Oh, it's you, my dear. I—er—don't know. He was not in the boat.'

'Oh,' said the girl and walking past them began to run down the hill.

The *Plover* was still lying at the landing jetty. She waved at the skipper.

'Are you sailing?'

'Ah'm not stayin' here,' he nodded at the eastern sky.

'Can you pop me aboard *Caryatid?*'

'I'd pop you in the club,' said a voice at her elbow and the skipper's grinning son helped her aboard.

'Sonia!' exclaimed Charlie when he saw her in the cabin doorway. They embraced, only to be interrupted by a knocking on the open door. They turned to find Bernard Foster. He looked irritable.

'I'm sorry, Mr Foster, I came on impulse, it's not Charlie's fault.' She smiled at him.

'Alright, but you must leave the instant I say. When I send the boat in for the crew. Alright?'

'Alright, thanks.'

Foster pulled the door closed after him. Yes, he did remember what it was like. And they faded so soon, these flowers.

Bernard Foster went up to the bridge. A quartermaster was polishing brass. He dogged his cigarette out. 'That's alright, Jones, don't worry.'

Foster peered out of the wheelhouse windows. The sea was getting up, following the increase of the wind. 'About force four to five,' volunteered the quartermaster.

'Mmmmm,' agreed the mate.

Not too bad, yet.

Aboard *Sea Dragon* the dining table pitched gently as the yacht became wind-rode. Stanier seemed not to notice it, but emptied his glass. At any rate no one remarked upon it as Sir Hector outlined his future plans to Pomeroy, Argyle and the newly accepted Stanier.

The women shuddered at the chill and retired into the smoke room where they chatted desultorily.

At the reeve's house the dinner was a contrast in couples. Justine and Macready made the best of it but they were clearly frustrated from expressing their innermost thoughts to each other.

Across the table the reeve and his wife were excitedly talking of the news their son had brought them. He had just made a great deal of money on a stock exchange deal and was in a position to buy them a house ashore. Because of his age and rheumatism the reeve was very tempted to take up his son's offer. His wife seemed delighted at the prospect of seeing her grandchildren regularly.

'Of course there'll be the question of a successor for you here, though,' said the Captain.

'Oh yes. That'll be the prerogative of his Lordship, of course. He may ask me to nominate someone suitable.'

'Tell me,' said Justine, 'tell me, do you have any cottages free at the moment? I was thinking of renting one on a more or less permanent basis.'

Beside her Macready held his breath. The evening was suddenly rosy again. Justine, Justine, is there no end to your sweetness?

Sonia sat alone in Charlie's cabin brushing her hair with her hand. Charlie was on the bridge, summoned by Bernard.

'It's backed nor'east and still freshening; once the wind-sea alters direction this anchorage'll be untenable. Get yourself ashore and round up the crew. And be quick about it!'

'Aye, aye, sir.' Charlie was off. He was suddenly alerted to potential danger.

Charlie burst into the reeve's house unannounced, Sonia at his heels. Macready knew instantly what was happening. A wind came in with the second mate that had the whip of malice in it.

Charlie, breathless, opened his mouth to speak.

'It's alright, Mr Farthing, I'm coming.' Sudden guilt seized the Captain as he turned to say his farewells. All he could impart to Justine was a look. Less even than he had thought he would manage that evening.

They were dancing and singing in the Craven Arms. The place was thick with the smoke of forty-odd cigarettes, loud with raucous shouts and noisy oaths. The whine of the accordion was drowned beneath the stamp of feet on the flagstones.

With a whoop Calico Jack leapt into the centre of the floor and whirled his ancient partner after him. The dance had no name beyond being the vertical expression of a horizontal desire. It reached a crescendo of noise and sweaty effort and Calico Jack stopped abruptly, jerking his partner to a halt.

The company fell silent as Sonia's

mother slipped the old fur coat from her thin shoulders and stood naked before the ship's company.

The door crashed open and a wind like a knife whipped into the bar. Charlie stood in the doorway.

'Caryatids out, down to the boat, move, come on, get some ginger into it!' He strode into the bar, thrusting men to their feet, trying desperately to infect these half-drunk bodies with his own sense of urgency.

'Come on! COME ON!'

Calico Jack pulled the fur coat back over the old woman's shoulders and smiled at her. She did not smile back.

The *Caryatid*'s crew stumbled out into the screaming darkness and Charlie drove them sheep-like down the hill.

Charlie never remembered how they got aboard the *Caryatid*. He remembered Sonia grabbing his neck and kissing him even as he thrust a greaser forwards. He remembered pulling a steward away from the edge of the precipitous drop that flanked one section of the path.

He remembered too the lights of *Caryatid* looming over them. Foster had got her underway to make a lee for the boat. Captain Macready was the last man to ascend the ladder. At the top he turned and shouted to Charlie.

'Mr Farthing, take the boat across to that yacht. Tell Stanier to get the hell out of this anchorage!'

'Aye, aye, sir.'

The boat turned away, swooping and dipping across the seas that now roared up out of the gathering gloom. Their sides were streaked with spume and their crests reared into breaking foam only to be whipped to shreds by the cutting wind. Charlie was soaked with the first sheet of spray that the boat flung up.

His leap across to the *Sea Dragon* was afterwards described with great admiration in the *Caryatid*'s mess deck by the boat's crew. Charlie burst into the smoke room where the women languidly lay about drinking. At his sudden, soaking appearance they squealed and started.

'Where's Stanier?' The reaction was blank. He strode wetly across the carpet and flung open the dining saloon door.

'What the hell d'you think—?' Stanier and Sir Hector rose protesting.

'Stanier! Get under way at once, man. There's a rising gale and you're on a lee shore!'

'How dare you, burst in here and—' Charlie waved Sir Hector to silence. He realised Stanier was half drunk.

Taking three strides over to the semi-recumbent form, Charlie grabbed his lapels and shook him. 'Stanier, get under WAY!'

Stanier shook his head. 'I've sheen you before. You're a damned insholent puppy from that bloody *Carya* ...' he stumbled over the name. 'Gerroff,' he tried plucking Charlie's fingers from his jacket. 'I ... I'm a Master Mariner, you damned scum.'

'You'll be bugger-all if you don't get off your arse!' Charlie dragged Stanier to his feet. The Harbour Master stood swaying. Charlie fetched him a swipe across his face.

'LEE SHORE!' he shouted at Stanier,

seeing the beginnings of alarm awaken in the puffily handsome features swaying before him.

Abruptly, frustratedly, Charlie walked out of the saloon.

'Playing sailor boys?' remarked Samantha from the depths of a leather armchair, then the intruder was gone into the windy gloom outside.

Pomeroy caught him as he stood poised to leap into the launch.

'Have we to move?'

Charlie turned. At last! Someone with a shred of sense aboard this useless toy boat. 'Yes! Get your anchor up and steam into it. Get Stanier to steam into the wind, d'you understand?' Pomeroy nodded. Spray soaked the pair of them as it lifted over *Sea Dragon*'s handsomely flared bow.

Charlie returned to *Caryatid*.

Darkness had almost descended onto the scene. The faintest glimmer of day threw up the loom of the island astern of them, then that too vanished. But the island remained outlined at its base where the waves dashed themselves to pieces in a roar that increased minute by minute.

High above the anchorage on the turn in the path which commanded a view of the bay, a little knot of figures gathered. The reeve accompanied Justine, and Sonia joined them, peering intently down into the darkness.

They watched as *Caryatid*'s lights swung beam on to the wind and she raced sideways towards the rocks. 'Picking up the launch ... ' explained the reeve, sucking in his breath. 'My God but I hope Macready knows what he's doing ...'

They watched as steam clouds caught the deck lights and the glimmer of figures on the boat-deck showed where furious activity was in progress.

The launch rose to the dripping boat deck as Macready fought *Caryatid* head to wind. Seamen rushed forward with lines to secure the boat. Foster stood, bawling orders, a black shiny figure in his oilskins. The launch swung inboard and down onto the chocks. Charlie scrambled out.

Up on the bridge he reported to the

Captain. 'Stanier's pissed, sir. I tried to tell them they're in danger. One of the men seemed to understand.' Macready looked across to where *Sea Dragon* still rode pitching to her anchor. At full speed ahead *Caryatid* was only passing her slowly. He rang 'Half Ahead' to keep the yacht under observation. A sea crashed over the *Caryatid*'s bow, deluging the foredeck with white water that glowed wickedly in the darkness. The foremast stood out of the swirl like a tree in a flooded field.

Caryatid shook herself, rose, and poured the unwanted water out over the side at the after end of the deck. Then she thumped into the next sea. It too thundered aft, with all the screaming demons of hell riding upon its crest. The wheelhouse windows shuddered at the impact of the gust. They were armoured glass.

Beyond the next two or three approaching seas visibility was negligible. Spume and spray smoked across the torn surface of the blackness, here and there a riven crest shredded away before it was half formed.

'Force Ten,' muttered Foster more to himself than anyone else. In the chartroom the barometer needle twitched as the next gust hit them.

'Only whores, thieves and sailors'd work on a night like this,' remarked the bosun to the carpenter as they each sucked a mug of tea in their messroom.

Aboard *Sea Dragon* Stanier staggered up to the little bridge. It was only when he got there he realised the danger the yacht was in. Because it was still a flood tide some local anomaly of the stream running north eastwards through the Hound's Teeth caused a deadening of the sea where *Sea Dragon* lay. But when the ebb got away ... Stanier shuddered, suddenly remembering Farthing's words: *'You'll have bugger-all if you don't get off your arse!'* Christ! Panic suddenly gripped his guts, shook his stomach and he spewed abruptly, violently, over the deck. His head cleared; he must make an effort. HE MUST. All his future lay before him, a mistake now ... if James St John

Stanier never knew humility this was his first taste of it.

He reached for the engine room telephone.

At that instant the anchor cable caught on an outlying projection of the Hound's Teeth. It sawed across the granite and snapped.

Sea Dragon fell into the trough of the sea. She began to drive inexorably to leeward and the waiting cliffs of Ynyscraven.

Aft in the smoke room the men joined the ladies. There was some idle chatter and mention of 'interesting visitors' and 'lee shores'. Caroline went forward to the wheelhouse. Half way along the alley-way she was thrown headlong as *Sea Dragon* slewed round.

Samantha's chair fell over and she was deposited, a leg-waving heap of frills, upon the thick carpet. Miss Loring began to scream. Argyle hit her. Sir Hector banged his head and out in the screaming darkness Pomeroy tried to get forward to see what was the matter. A wave washed him aft but, with a superhuman effort he made the wheelhouse door and opened it.

Pomeroy skidded in the vomit. Stanier was heaving the wheel over. From below came the rumble of a diesel starting. The aspirated air hissed from the funnel and the engine fired. Stanier breathed a sigh of relief. Soon, soon *Sea Dragon* had to turn ...

The *Caryatid*'s officers watched as the *Sea Dragon* drove down wind. She rolled abominably so that they could see her boot topping in contrast with her white sides.

After a minute or so Macready said flatly, 'She's had it.'

No one disagreed with him.

Down in the boiler room of the *Caryatid*, Calico Jack plied his shovel and raked ash. With the nimbleness of years he countered the pitch of the ship. Turn, shovel, turn, fling. He stopped, wiped his gleaming brow and clanged the boiler door shut with his foot. A sudden heaviness seized him. A pain in his chest opened before him like a huge red flower. He plunged into it and its bloody petals folded round him.

High above the two struggling ships, barely heard in the wind's howl, a not so very old woman screamed. The sound was caught by the cliffs in the diminuendo of swift descent.

Sea Dragon began to gather headway.

Before he could get her to answer her helm the motor yacht drove southwards, still rolling across the wind but gathering the momentum needed for her rudder to bite.

She began to turn ...

'She's turning,' yelled Stanier at the white faced Pomeroy.

Sea Dragon began to bring her head to the east.

Then the Hound's Teeth found her bottom.

Aftermath

The rocket blazed up into the night and hung like a ruby star before falling seawards slowly.

There was nothing those aboard *Caryatid* could do until daylight.

'They'll just have to hang on.' Macready spoke for them all. *Caryatid* was having her own problems keeping head to sea. The sudden collapse of one of the firemen had caused a temporary loss of steam and Macready had endured a quarter of an hour of extreme anxiety before he had conned the old ship back onto a safe heading.

'It's Evans, sir,' reported Foster. 'He's had what looks like a heart attack.'

'Which Evans, Bernard?' asked Macready patiently, never taking his eyes from the next sea rising massively ahead of his little—oh so little—ship.

'Calico Jack, Captain, we've got him out of the boiler room but he's quite dead.'

'I'm sorry about that.' Macready watched the sea. 'Starboard, midships, steadeeeeee.' The sea exploded over the bow and the whole ship trembled.

'What's the light-bearing now, Mr Farthing?'

'Two five eight, sir.'

'Magnetic or True?'

'True, sir.'

'Good. I wonder if there's any chance of some tea?'

Sea Dragon drove onto the rocks as each succeeding sea raised her up and smashed her down again. She lay on her beam ends, her steel hull screaming a protest as the Hound's Teeth ripped at her guts and the sea, like some monstrous tongue, ground her down on the granite molars.

Aboard her all was terror and confusion. There were no lights and loose gear flew about indiscriminately. Water sloshed up and down alley-ways and passengers and crew scrabbled mercilessly at one another.

Stanier did what he could. The other anchor was let go to try and prevent the yacht from driving further up the reef, he sent off the rockets and an SOS on the radio, but a sea-drenched aerial about a fathom from the surface of the waves was of little use.

It was Pomeroy who organised them. Despised Pomeroy who at last found some shred of use from an education that had otherwise blighted his life. Calm, unhurried, he organised the crew and passengers into groups to check on lifesaving appliances and the chances of organising some food and keeping warm. Anything to pass the night. When Stanier thought of the same thing he found Pomeroy had beaten him to it.

Pomeroy earned the grudging admiration of even Samantha when the whole group, sheltered in the main alley-way, each adorned in a bulky lifejacket, were sipping rum toddy.

Up in the wheelhouse Sir Hector stood watching his yacht disintegrate.

'Will she hold till daylight?' He turned to

look at Stanier. The yacht's young master was ashen-faced. He had no experience to base his answer on. Would she? *Sea Dragon* gave a sickening lurch as a huge sea broke over her and the Hound's Teeth.

'My God—' Sir Hector slipped in the slick of vomit that now smeared the greater part of the *Sea Dragon*'s wheelhouse deck. He fell with a crash, his head striking the wheel mounting. Blood spurted and he rolled concussed into the lee corner as Stanier stood stock still, bracing himself for the onslaught of the next wave which, by its delay, he knew instinctively was enormous.

The sea which hit *Sea Dragon* rolled roaring up the reef, hummocking itself into a furious entity baulked by the granite barrier. Its outriders ran left and right into a hundred gullies and fissures, boiling with energy. As the impeding rocks sapped the momentum below, its crest rushed on, driven forward by its impetus yet undermined of its own support. As it toppled over and collapsed in a moil of spent energy it burst into the yacht. Her boats were swept away by the funnel as it imploded, vanishing into the night. The cowl vents disappeared and ton after ton of salt water roared down into the alley-way. Bodies were washed screaming and kicking up and down like flotsam.

Eventually the water subsided and *Sea Dragon* seemed to have settled, to be moving less. The waves seemed less powerful.

Stanier moved across to Sir Hector.

Sir Hector Blackadder was dead. Stanier turned away, his stomach heaving again. He stumbled aft, making for the alley-way where he knew the others were.

Pomeroy had got them on their feet and was tallying them.

Horrocks was missing, so too were Tegwyn and Samantha. Caroline pointed aft. The door to the saloon and smoke room was smashed. Caroline struggled towards it, Pomeroy and Stanier followed.

Water impeded their movements, difficult enough with the vessel lying on her beam ends. They found Tegwyn in the corner of the smoke room, an armchair on top of her. The two men pulled it off. She lay like a dropped marionette. Even in distress Pomeroy drew in his breath at her beauty. Stanier felt sudden revulsion at the incongruity of her sprawled body. The two men exchanged glances then Pomeroy, his face white with strain, lowered his head onto her bosom.

'She's alive, and only unconscious.' Grunting with effort they dragged Tegwyn into a sitting position. Pomeroy found a bottle of cognac and forced it between her lips.

Stanier regarded the open door to the quarterdeck. No glass remained in it. Was that where Samantha and Horrocks had gone? They found Horrocks by accident. A lurch of the *Sea Dragon* swung open a water closet door. Inside lay Horrocks, driven into a foetal curve around the porcelain pan, his head and hand cut and his dignity disposed of, but alive. They dragged him out into the alley-way where the others huddled. Of Samantha there was no sign.

'She's easier now, skipper,' said the

bosun. Stanier nodded silently, wiping the rime of white saliva from the corners of his mouth. He did not even notice the man's use of the fishing boat term.

'Anyone else hurt?' he managed at last.

A few cuts and several bruises were displayed. Miss Loring hid her head. Caroline was bent over her.

'What's the matter with her?' asked Stanier.

Caroline looked up. 'Poor Dot's lost two of her front teeth.' Miss Loring wailed pitifully.

Stanier suddenly remembered the corpse in the wheelhouse.

'Where's Argyle?'

'Here, laddie.' The Gael looked much older than he had a few hours earlier. Stanier took him up to the wheelhouse.

'Oh my God!' said Argyle bending over his friend. 'If ah wasna' a hard heided business mon ah'd swear he'd a premonition o' his death.'

'We'll have to tell Caroline.'

'Tell Caroline? Oh, sweet Christ!'

The girl came forward and bent over her

father, cradling his head in her arms.

Argyle plucked Stanier's sleeve and they descended to the alley-way.

'Captain,' said Pomeroy at last. 'What are our chances?'

Stanier bowed under the responsibility. Why the hell did they keep asking bloody silly questions? Then he recollected himself. Dammit, he *was* master. A picture of the ever confident Macready in this situation sent the blood to his head. Macready!

'I hope *Caryatid*'ll get a boat to us in the morning. In the meantime we must make the best of this.' A thought dawned on him. 'The ebb tide's away, that's why we're no longer pounding. We'll be high and dry at daylight.'

An hour before daylight the wind began to veer. On *Caryatid*'s bridge a monotonous routine of position fixing and course checking had culminated in the information that in something under six and a half hours the steamer had made four miles offing from the island. Everyone on board was dog tired.

Macready turned from the window. 'Bernard?'

'Sir?'

'This wind's sou'east, it's low water. There'll be the beginnings of a lee in the anchorage at Ynyscraven. If we aren't there at daylight we'll have precious little chance of getting those poor bastards off that yacht once the flood makes.'

'No, sir.'

'We are going to have to turn round. Go down and let everyone know they're to hang on. Don't forget the engine room. Do it personally.'

'Aye, aye, sir.'

Charlie watched Foster go below. The man had not rested for hours, constantly patrolling the ship to check on damage, closures, personnel.

When the Mate returned to the bridge, Macready seemed to gather himself, draw in his breath and with it the whole wheelhouse seemed to contract ready for some muscular spasm.

The Captain was the lonely lord now, staring out into the furious night, perhaps two hundred crew and their dependants waiting on his judgement and his alone.

Macready watched the sea. *Caryatid* plunged through an enormous wave and Macready banged the telegraphs to 'Full Ahead'. *Caryatid* gathered speed, hoisting the next wave over her battered foredeck so that, with the increased impetus, it hit the bridge front with a shuddering thump and exploded over the wings in a white hiss. *Caryatid*'s bow lurched out of the wave and hung over the trough, then she plunged downwards, pounding into the next sea and flinging that too over her funnel. Then her motion eased. Behind the big, cumulative waves came the lull.

'Hard a-starboard!'

'Hard a-starboard, sir.' Charlie watched the wheelspokes spin in the dim light of the binnacle. 'Wheel's hard a-starboard, sir.' *Caryatid* began her turn.

The reeve's house became a kind of headquarters for the island's insomniacs that night. Sonia was there with Justine and half a dozen other people. The off-duty keepers from the lighthouse had struggled down across the wind-torn island to assist as they could when they had seen the red flare go skywards from the *Sea Dragon*. For the first time the name of the yacht that had been lying in the bay was mentioned. When Justine heard it confirmed that it was, in fact, Sir Hector Blackadder's yacht, fear for her daughter overwhelmed her. It was fear laced with guilt and a deep Celtic submission to divine retribution that lit her beautiful eyes with sorrow. She felt now the inevitability of the train of events, how the idyll with Septimus must be paid for in the same total currency with which it had been enjoyed.

At dawn one of the shepherds came down from the high ground with the news that he thought the *Caryatid* was approaching the island. There was a disbelieving exodus from the reeve's house. Wearing sheepskins Justine and Sonia held hands against the wind and struggled out to the cliff path. Justine shrieked her fears for her daughter into the gale and Sonia squeezed her hand in comprehension.

The gale was easing as it veered. For a while they could see nothing in the grey murk. As the sky lightened they made out the white, broken shape of the *Sea Dragon* lying on the black rocks below them and out to their right.

'There she is!' shouted Sonia, pointing. Justine's heart beat wildly at the scene. The waves still marched into the anchorage in long lines, streaked with white. Their crests still crashed remorselessly upon the granite bulk of the island and if they did so with less venom than earlier, it took a seaman of Macready's experience to detect the difference. To the two women the anchorage still looked a fearsome place. Then they saw the steamer. *Caryatid* seemed to race towards the island, scending in the following sea. The black smoke from her funnel blew forward, advancing before her as the wind whipped it along the sea surface mixing its sulphurous stink with the clean white spume.

'He's either very brave or mad, your captain,' shouted Sonia, squeezing Justine's hand again reassuringly.

'What's he going to do?' asked the elder woman, scarcely able to believe her beloved Septimus was, like Lancelot, coming to the rescue. 'He's coming straight at the cliffs!'

Sonia shrugged. 'I don't know.'

They watched *Caryatid* drive into the anchorage past *Sea Dragon*. They were unaware that Macready's sea-sense told him that with a veering wind there *must* be a point just under the lee of the Hound's Teeth that would allow him to launch a boat.

Charlie walked along the boat deck as the hands swung the launch out-board. Mackerel Jack and his crew looked apprehensive. Charlie stared out over the port side. The cliffs of Ynyscraven were looming inexorably closer. He could see lights still in the windows of the reeve's house and there, on the path ... was that a patch of russet?

Caryatid forged ahead even with stopped engines. Macready shook his head to clear the fatigue from his brain. He had to get this manoeuvre right. Sensing the moment was correct he slammed the starboard engine telegraph to 'Full Ahead' and blew the whistle, yelling out 'Hard a-port!'

At the signal the carpenter forward let go the port anchor and on the boat-deck the launch started its jerky descent to the roaring sea.

Justine watched spellbound while Sonia jumped up and down, so great was the tension. *Caryatid* turned, almost snatched herself round as her anchor cable bit into the hawse-pipe and smoke rose blue from her elm-block capstan brakes. She hung a moment broadside to the wind and sea, rolled down, up and down again.

'Hooks!' roared Foster as the boat was slipped into the wave, then *Caryatid* rolled again, away from the boat.

Charlie gasped as the engine coughed and fired. The boat shot from the lee of the steamer as *Caryatid* snubbed her cable head to wind and began to heave it in again.

Minutes later Charlie was scrambling ashore on the land-ward end of the Hound's Teeth where the wind effect was lost and the sea, emasculated by the reef, was no more than a surging nuisance to a fit man.

Up on the cliff Sonia saw who it was that scrambled ashore and turned to Justine with shining eyes. 'Charlie's there, Justine! Charlie's there!'

She put her arm round Justine for the older woman was crying, partly from relief, partly from love and partly from a terrible apprehension.

Under normal circumstances none of the passengers and few of the crew of the *Sea Dragon* would have undertaken that 'walk' ashore to safety. It was a nightmare journey of stumbling and wallowing in rock pools a fathom deep; of scrambling cut and bruised over granite and shale fissured by the sea and sharp with shell-fish. Oar weed tore at their legs and the trembling rocks shook with the impact of the sea not a dozen yards away from them. But the launch picked them up and landed them at last on the store jetty. Up at the reeve's house they were dried out and fed and made to get some rest. About mid-afternoon, the wind having gone to the south and moderated still further, *Caryatid* finally anchored safely and the survivors trooped out to be accommodated aboard the ship.

Charlie and Mackerel Jack and the boat's crew made no attempt to regain the ship after rescuing the *Sea Dragon*'s people until *Caryatid* returned. Macready had been specific upon this point, ordering Charlie to sacrifice the boat rather than run the further risk of attempting a recovery in a place not of his, Macready's, choosing.

It was evening when the survivors were all on board and Captain Macready, tired though he was, ordered the ship under way for Porth Ardur. Clear of the island he rang down 'Slow Ahead'.

'We'll arrive at daybreak,' he explained.

Such was the combination of guilt and dread in the soul of Justine Morgan that to find Tegwyn alive was nearly as much of a shock as if she had received what she conceived to be her inevitable deserts. Her solicitude for her bruised and battered daughter was fulsome by way of compensation; though whether to propitiate the deities or ease her own conscience was uncertain. In her relief Justine was magnificent in bringing comfort to all the survivors of the *Sea Dragon* and, as their ministering angel, it did not seem unnatural that she should take passage with them in *Caryatid*.

Aboard the steamer Justine stayed close to her daughter who, still in a state of shock, did not seem surprised to find her mother suddenly on the scene of disaster. The survivors were accommodated in the officers' saloon and Justine herself asked no questions when a smooth, oiled, yet pleasantly attentive young man paid court to Tegwyn. Justine kept well out of Macready's way and was content to be on his ship and making herself useful.

Caroline had said very little to Stanier during the entire incident of the grounding. Aboard *Caryatid*, however, she drew Argyle aside and talked at some length with him. About ten o'clock that night, as *Caryatid* wallowed along at slow speed, she sought Stanier out.

He too had kept himself to himself after the disaster. His world lay in ruins about his feet. His pride and aspirations, so readily buoyed up, so recently at a zenith of scarcely-imagined promise, lay dashed to fragments upon the evil line of the Hound's Teeth.

He leant on the rail gazing astern where the swells dipped and lifted, still angry but dying as the wind dropped away.

'Hullo, Jimmy,' said Caroline gently.

'Caroline?' There was a catch in his voice that betrayed him. Was it grief or self-pity?

'Oh, Caro, your father ... I ...' he began to weep. She held out her arms.

'Come, come, Jimmy, don't say the witch Tegwyn has unmanned you completely.'

He looked at her. There was no grief in her face. He sniffed inelegantly. She kissed him full on the lips. After a little he responded as she summoned his virility from its own tight coil of misery.

'Oh, Jimmy, life has to go on, you know,

it has to go on and we can make it change direction.'

James St John Stanier, late master of the motor yacht *Sea Dragon*, ground his hips into the pelvis of the daughter, the wicked daughter, of the late and unlamented Sir Hector Blackadder.

Tegwyn and Stanier never said another word to each other. It was as though that final wave that had crashed aboard *Sea Dragon* had extinguished forever the fierce heat of their affair. The lovely Tegwyn, who had bruised a rib in her headlong, water-propelled flight along the alley-way, gave herself willingly to the ministrations of her mother and the gentle Pomeroy. She accepted his proposal before *Caryatid* turned the point and brought the grey-green mountain of Mynydd Uchaf ahead.

Return of the Argonauts

Long before Mr Marconi harnessed them, radio waves were crackling through the ether. It was by some telepathic link utilising this phenomenon that news of *Caryatid*'s doings always seemed to arrive in Porth Ardur ahead of the ship.

It is true that Macready sent in a message via the Coast Guard, but it was brief and without details. Afterwards there were many who swore they knew that *Caryatid* was coming in with survivors before she had even left Ynyscraven.

Gwendolen Macready spent the evening during which Tegwyn Morgan was accepting Pomeroy's proposal of marriage and Stanier was accepting Caroline's proposal of God knows what, in organising the church hall for the reception of the victims of shipwreck. She mobilised half the women-folk of the town into a sort of trench kitchen which had enough blankets, soup and tea for a small brigade of the regular army, and was on the quay when *Caryatid* berthed. It was the first time in ten years that she had been this near the ship. It was not, of course, to meet her husband that she stood thus in the windy morning, but to organise the unfortunate in their misery. She saw the huddle of figures waiting for the gangway to give them access to *terra firma* and among them she saw Justine Morgan.

Now Gwendolen had absolutely no knowledge of how Justine had got aboard the *Caryatid,* nor is it certain that, although she knew Mrs Morgan's shop had been closed for some days and that Mrs Morgan was not on the guest list of the *Sea Dragon* while her daughter was, her brain went through any logical process of deduction at the moment when she saw Justine. But like St Paul on the road to Damascus she suddenly knew. Knew everything. Her intuition flashed, long held suspicions, idle gossip, her own feeling of justified martyrdom, all suddenly crystallised into certainty.

But being who she was, she first had work to do.

The survivors allowed themselves to be marshalled into the church hall and kitted out in badly fitting clothes. Tegwyn and Justine slipped quietly home. After receiving dry gear, Stanier and Caroline drove to the house in Glendŵr Avenue while the others made their way to the Station Hotel and those of the crew who had not already done so and lived locally, also drifted home.

That night Caroline permitted Stanier to sleep with her, but only after he had resigned as Harbour Master of Porth Ardur.

Captain Macready was very tired when he eventually got home. Already the mental exertions of the rescue had reduced a guilt he might otherwise have felt on first encountering his wife after a week in another's arms. His exhaustion was too obvious for Gwendolen to take advantage of, and in any case she was too cautious a person to mistime a scene in which the full savour of her martyrdom could be enjoyed. Wronged women not only have justice on their side, but can also choose when to gratify the last shreds of departing pride.

Pomeroy called on Justine and Tegwyn before his train left the following morning.

'Will you come up to town soon, my dear?' he asked Tegwyn. 'Your trousseau will receive my personal attention. You will lack nothing a truly feminine heart could desire.' He smiled, a degree of confidence in his bearing that had not been there before the night *Sea Dragon* pounded herself to pieces upon the Hound's Teeth.

'Yes, of course. Mother has decided to sell the shop if she can find a cottage on Ynyscraven.'

Pomeroy turned towards Justine in surprise. 'You want to return to that Godforsaken rock, Mrs Morgan?'

Justine smiled at him. 'If I can be sure that you'll take care of Tegwyn.'

Pomeroy returned her smile. 'I shall

do more than that. I shall adore her as my dearest treasure.' He paused. 'And Mrs Morgan, I would be pleased to help financially with the cottage.'

Justine looked at him. There was no diffidence about him, no embarrassment. He was a rich man, a rich and confident man, and Tegwyn was smiling delightedly.

There was little more to say after that fulsome speech.

In the train, Argyle travelled up to town with Miss Loring and Caroline. Pomeroy joined them before the train pulled out of Porth Ardur but said little during the journey. Dorothy Loring hid her face in a scarf and felt wretched. She would never, ever travel again. It might broaden the mind but it had ruined her looks. Argyle was aggressively articulate though, half whispering when he remembered, half shouting when he forgot, remonstrating with a cool, determined Caroline.

'But in heaven's name *why*, Caroline? The man's bluidy nearly responsible for the death of us all. He's certainly morally responsible for the death of your father. What possible asset will he be now to Blackadder Holdings and the Cambrian Steam Navigation Company?'

'Don't be a fool, Ian. Who's morally responsible for my mother's health, or lack of it? D'you think I mourn the old tyrant? Oh, I know you liked him and I know others admired him, but I could never forgive him for those painted trollops with the airs of duchesses that he used to tow around.'

'But Caroline, your ain Stanier's nae different.'

'My Stanier's *very* different. I'll be pulling the strings, don't you worry, but out front, where Cambrian and Blackadder need a good, impressive public image, that's where Jimmy Stanier will be.' Caroline licked her lips. Besides, he was not without certain technical accomplishments.

Argyle sat back with a sigh. 'Och dammit! I ken well your father liked him ...'

Caroline seized the point. 'Exactly! If he

fooled Father he can fool the world.' She paused. 'How d'you like the name 'Argyle and Blackadder', Ian?'

'What exactly are you planning?' Argyle asked, his interest rekindled and redirected.

Caroline smiled as the train plunged into a tunnel.

On Ynyscraven Sonia had watched *Caryatid* fade into the distance. She returned sadly to the cottage and wondered why her mother was still absent. It was not unusual for her mother to be missing, but there was a vague worry forming in the back of her mind.

Next day the body of Samantha came ashore in the little cove beneath the coombe. The long blonde hair floated like weed about the once lovely, disdainful face. A herring gull had already found her eyes but even in disfigured death she still possessed something of that lissome beauty that had attracted the experienced attention of Sir Hector Blackadder. Sonia saw the body as they brought it up for burial. The reeve, as the island's coroner, forwarded a report for the formal inquiry at Porth

Ardur. They never found Sonia's mother, despite an island-wide search. Sonia felt sad at the death of the old woman, little grief but a deep sense of pity and relief at the mercy of death for the old and shattered soul.

Out on the Hound's Teeth the first gales of September churned the white plating of *Sea Dragon* into a rusting mass of red oxidisation. The wreck slowly yet inexorably lost the appearance of a ship. By Christmas she looked as if she had once been a lean-to stable made of rusty iron. She had become merely another victim of the iron-bound coast of Ynyscraven.

By the spring, the reeve had made definite plans to leave the island. He spoke to Sonia about the possibility of sharing her cottage with another lady.

Sonia had asked who, and the reeve had replied that he had received a request from Mrs Morgan of Porth Ardur for the first vacant cottage. Sonia eagerly jumped at the idea.

'I would love to have her here,' she

replied, her eyes catching fire, 'at least until I'm married.'

Justine arrived in the *Plover* a month later. Sonia was delighted to see her. She looked older, less buoyant. She had slipped the wrong side of middle age during the winter, but she was still a handsome woman.

'The *Plover*'s crew are talking of the Earl coming down soon to appoint a new reeve,' she told Sonia. 'D'you think Charlie would be interested?'

'Charlie?' Sonia was thunderstruck. 'Why-I-er-good heavens I never thought ...'

'You'll have to talk it over with him next time *Caryatid* comes here.'

'Oh, what an idea, Justine. That would be marvellous ... I never thought of that.'

Charlie had no idea of the plans being hatched for him on Ynyscraven. He was content to visit the island as often as *Caryatid* called and to plan for a future of bliss with the lovely Sonia. He had attended the inquiry into the loss of the *Sea Dragon* and the consequent deaths.

Oddly it was his and Macready's evidence that saved Stanier's professional certificate. Partly out of guilt, partly out of truth, Macready testified that the gale had been exceptionally fierce, arrived with no warning and been devastating in its effect. He explained the ease with which *Caryatid*, a steamer with steam constantly on her boilers and manned professionally could weigh her anchor faster than a motor yacht. He ignored Stanier's pained look, aware that he had it in his power to destroy the younger man. Charlie did not volunteer the information that Stanier was drunk and was not asked. As a consequence the stranding was adjudged 'an accident' and the deaths recorded as by 'misadventure'. Poor Calico Jack's was recorded as due to a coronary thrombosis and his shipmates mourned his loss as only sailors can. They bemoaned the hardship that now compelled one of their number to turn-to early and prepare *Caryatid*'s boilers for sea.

No one saw the going of Stanier. He passed quietly from the scene, regretted only by the wives who had found in him an ally against the smoking funnel of the *Caryatid*.

Charlie heard later that on the recommendation of Captain Macready, Thomas Jones was appointed temporary harbour master of Porth Ardur and that either Stan or Fred were often to be seen mowing the Captain's lawn or weeding his herbaceous borders.

It was only after the inquiry that Gwendolen Macready felt the moment ripe for her outburst. She sat knitting by the fire. The chimney smoked into the room as a gust of wind blew down it. Opposite, her husband sat dozing, unaware that the smell reminded Gwendolen of an *auto da fé*.

'Septimus,' she said.

He woke. 'Uh?' he stretched. 'What is it?'

'Now that all the unpleasantness of the inquests is over I can talk to you about your behaviour recently.' Macready jerked awake. 'Don't argue with me. I've been aware for some time that what went on between you and that Mrs Morgan was very unpleasant for me, has made me the laughing stock of the town ... please don't deny it. I've been in correspondence with the reeve's wife and reading between the lines ... well, it's not very pleasant is it? I believe that Mrs Morgan's gone to live permanently on the island and I suppose that means that you'll be ... that you and she ...'

Gwendolen had prepared all the speech down to the last detail but now, in her moment of agony she could not betray her dignity to utter crudities. She faltered.

Macready, who had listened open-mouthed, urged her mentally on. Go on, he thought, say it.

'... you'll be seeing her there.' Gwendolen managed at last.

Macready sat up, carefully choosing his words, making his case as plaintive as possible. 'I did not mean to cause you any pain, my dear, but we've never been very close in bed.'

'Septimus! You really are disgusting! Now listen to me. I intend to remain your wife and continue as I always have in this town.' She gave a heroic little sniff that Macready found quite incongruously appealing, reminding him of a certain cast of her head that once, long years ago, he had found attractive. He stifled a smile.

'I shall expect the highest standards of propriety from you while you are here. If I do not receive them I shall make a fuss.' She uttered this with an air of quite terrifying finality. She had fired her broadside and Macready knew the ammunition in it was enough, at least in Gwendolen's opinion, to destroy him. By 'fuss' Gwendolen intimated in her euphemistic way that she would institute divorce proceedings. It would hurt her, he mused, far more than it would hurt him. But he must capitulate, touched as much with pity as guilt. 'I am truly sorry, my dear, to distress you.'

He hung his head like a chastised schoolboy.

Gwendolen sniffed, the gleam of triumph in her eyes. 'That's all there is to say on the subject. If you keep your side of the bargain I shall not mention the matter again.'

Macready sank back in his chair. Across the infinite divide of the hearth rug his marriage held together on agreement. Like the perfect railway lines it so resembled.

On her side of the hearth Gwendolen stilled her beating heart. Now she could really organise the town with her husband to loyally back her, not questioning any decision she might make in wielding his not inconsiderable influence. She had received his proxy and was ready once again to enter the lists around the parish pump from where his actions had besmirched her right to champion just causes.

Gwendolen Macready felt the exquisite agony of burning at a self-ignited stake.

Justine looked up from the table where she had been reading. Sonia lay asleep on her bed. Justine wondered about Tegwyn, whom she had last seen wrapped in silk and furs like a movie star, looking lovelier and happier than ever. She put down her book and walked quietly over to gaze down at the girl. The russet hair spilled out across the pillow, the darker lashes lay closed on the high, Slavic cheekbones

Beneath her blouse the girl's breasts rose and fell rhythmically. Justine regarded her for a long time, then she bent and pulled a blanket up over the recumbent form. Returning to the table she blew out the light.

A full, yellow moon sent its beams into the old cottage. The wind moaned softly in the chimney. Justine slipped out of her clothes and into bed. She lay on her back staring out of the window. She wondered if she too, like Sonia's mother, would go mad in this eldritch place.

Caryatid steamed south west. Astern the blue hummock of Mynydd Uchaf faded into the distance. The sea sparkled blue and banks of cumulo-nimbus rose ahead, their heads shearing off into anvils.

Captain Septimus Macready paced his bridge. His brass-bound uniform caught the sunlight, twinkling with pride. Macready thought of Stanier and wondered where he had got to. He remembered the ugly scene when Stanier had accused him of being a charlatan. He chuckled to himself.

He, Captain Septimus Macready, was the real sailor, Stanier a mere stuffed shirt gigolo! He alone remained the pre-eminent nautical figure in Porth Ardur. Why, thought the Captain sniffing the briny air happily, had he not left one wife sitting by her hearth fire in Porth Ardur? And was he not even now steaming towards another waiting patiently for him upon his own enchanted isle?

PERTH AND KINROSS LIBRARIES

The publishers hope that this book has given you enjoyable reading. Large Print Books are especially designed to be as easy to see and hold as possible. If you wish a complete list of our books, please ask at your local library or write directly to: Magna Large Print Books, Long Preston, North Yorkshire, BD23 4ND, England.

This Large Print Book for the Partially sighted, who cannot read normal print, is published under the auspices of

THE ULVERSCROFT FOUNDATION

THE ULVERSCROFT FOUNDATION

. . . we hope that you have enjoyed this Large Print Book. Please think for a moment about those people who have worse eyesight problems than you . . . and are unable to even read or enjoy Large Print, without great difficulty.

You can help them by sending a donation, large or small to:

**The Ulverscroft Foundation,
1, The Green, Bradgate Road,
Anstey, Leicestershire, LE7 7FU,
England.**

or request a copy of our brochure for more details.

The Foundation will use all your help to assist those people who are handicapped by various sight problems and need special attention.

Thank you very much for your help.